DEANNE
IN THE MIDDLE

Other books by DuEwa Frazier

Goddess Under the Bridge: Poems (2013)

Ten Marbles and a Bag to Put Them In: Poems for Children (2010)

Check the Rhyme: An Anthology of Female Poets & Emcees (2006)

Stardust Tracks on a Road (2005)

Shedding Light From My Journeys (2002)

Deanne in the Middle

By

DuEwa Frazier

Lit Noire Publishing

New York

Published by Lit Noire Publishing

www.duewaworld.com

Copyright © 2007—2014 DuEwa Frazier, DuEwa M. Frazier

Library of Congress Control Number: 2014911069

Deanne in the middle / DuEwa Frazier.

ISBN-13: 9780971905290 (paperback)

For all of my English teachers
For the nerds, geeks and "Oreos"
And for Maya Angelou—Rest in peace

ACKNOWLEDGEMENTS

I wrote *Deanne in the Middle* for every teen who has experienced being called "a nerd," "a geek," and a "wannabe." We often hear about the struggles of children who live in both urban and suburban environments who aren't expected to speak a certain way, look a certain way and perform at a certain academic level. This story is for them.

I champion the identity and unique backgrounds of all children and challenge teachers, youth and institutions to foster unity and an inclusive environment. Bullying does not just happen in middle America or to kids who are "quiet" it happens to all children—smart, black, confident, braniac, hip, nerdy, punk, etc.

Thank you to my family for their continued support. Thanks to all of the students I have worked with over the years. Thanks for the inspiration and encouragement from fellow writers Angela Jackson Brown, Danette Vigilante, Jeff Rivera, R. Kayeen Thomas and Kelly Starling Lyons. Special thanks to: Lisa Goldstein at The Brooklyn Public Library, Rob Bautista of The Funky Writer Show and the graduate writing program at The New School.

Day in and day out I can't seem to get you off my back. What do you think I should do about that?

~Monie Love, "Monie in the Middle"

CHAPTER 1
NEW BEGINNING

"IF YOU WANT THIS LIFE YOU GONNA HAVE TO WORK GIRL! DANCE DEANNE! DANCE GIRL!" I wake up breathing heavy like I just finished running for my life. More like dancing for my life. Sweat is dripping down my forehead and I'm drenched all over. Not the best way to wake up. I can still hear the voice of Debbie Allen, my dance idol, in my ear. *Dance girl dance!* It was only a dream.

It's the first day of school. I'm already feeling excited and anxious. *Dance girl dance!* Stonywood High here I come. And now what to wear? The name of the game in high school is dress to impress. Why should I be any different?

Getting out of my bed is a must right now. I look around my room, yeah it's a complete mess. The mess doesn't motivate me. My closet is regurgitating all of my t-shirts, sweaters, shorts, skirts, belts and jackets falling out of it. I don't have enough closet or drawer space. It's really time for a new room. Or I have to give some things away. I'm organized, but in a chaotic way. I know where everything is and that's what counts. I think I'll wear my black Juicy Couture jeans and a black and white Ed Hardy T-shirt. I'm set.

A girl isn't complete without a luxurious bath and pampering. My smell good potion and elixirs for my first day will be Selena Gomez Vivamore bath and shower gel, followed by Vivamore lotion and perfume spray.

Hair is easy. I wear it in a wrap style. All I have to do is comb my wrap, put a little moisture on and wallah magic! My shoulder length hair lays smooth and flat as long as it's not too humid outside. Now my hair plus humidity that's another story. I don't have a relaxer so edge and frizz control is definitely an issue at times. My hair will curl up on a hot day. Now for make-up. I don't wear much. Just a little Clinique gloss in Sunset and black Maybelline eyeliner. No blush. No messy mascara. I don't know how girls put all of that on. They call it "beating face." Who wants a face that looks beat? Not me. I want a fresh face.

Getting myself ready is pretty simple, but getting my younger sister Darlene dressed and ready—that's another story. I'm fourteen and Darlene is ten. She's smart and cute, but difficult. Time to wake her up.

"Darlene what are you doing? Time to get ready."

"Deanne, please!" Darlene pulls the covers back over her head. "I'm trying to get a little more sleep."

"Time to get up and get dressed."

"I don't know what to wear. You pick it out."

See what did I tell you? Darlene = difficult. And whiny. I'm always big sister to the rescue.

"This looks good. Pink cardigan over a turquoise t-shirt with denim skirt."

"Fine," Darlene says.

"Now get up Darlene."

While Darlene heads to the bathroom I organize her backpack. Notebooks, binder, pens, pencil and personal organizer. Oh, can't forget her cell phone and charger, and her pre-packed lunch bag mom made, which is downstairs. After Darlene comes out the bathroom, it's time for another round of beauty shop.

"Dar', let me help with your hair."

"I'll plug the curling iron in and really hook you up."

"No, no." Darlene snaps, as she gets dressed. "Last time you burned me Deanne! I'll do it."

"Dar' I know why you're always running late and doing what you want, when you want. You're spoiled!"

"Whatever." Darlene says sarcastically.

"As long as I'm getting both of us out in the morning for the rest of the year—you'd better behave."

Heading back to my room. I need to do a double check to make sure I don't forget anything. I have to pack my own bag and make sure my phone is charged up.

I grab my bag and phone and walk downstairs. I brush against the bookshelf near the kitchen door. A photo falls from one of the shelves. It's an old picture of my mom and dad. Mom comes from behind me.

"Deanne, what are you looking at?" Mom asks.

"An old picture of you and daddy."

"It must've fallen out of the album," she says. "You know I haven't heard from your father since I contacted his lawyer about him not paying any child support. Put the picture back and get ready for school."

I hold the photo in my hands. My parents sure look young and happy. This is before my father left us to pursue his career as an actor. He used to be an attorney and when mom got pregnant with Darlene, my dad suddenly had an epiphany—he needed to fulfill his childhood dream of being an actor before it was "too late." He said he hated law and he wanted out. So he quit his job and he left us. Moved to L.A. to become a big star. He could have still been an actor with a family. Guess he didn't think so. Mom has never really explained it to me. Other than to say, "He wasn't ready to commit to his family for life. The pressures were just too much for him." What does that mean? Me and Darlene are no "pressure" just two girls. And from what I hear, girls aren't nearly as much as a handful as boys are.

I'm feeling sad and angry too. Angry because my dad copped out and left us for no good reason, at all. Well he had a reason, his own selfish reason. If dad were here, mom wouldn't have to work so hard. Mom always says "don't dwell on the past," so I won't—today. I wish my dad was here to see me start my first day of high school. I go into the kitchen with breakfast on my mind: wheat toast, turkey bacon, scrambled eggs with cheese and orange juice. I whip it all up and serve it on plates.

"Breakfast is ready Darlene. Come down and eat. You don't want to be late for Uncle John to picking you up."

"You're so annoying this morning," Darlene says. "I'm coming."

Now that we're both ready, time to head out and see if this day will be amazing or a complete flop. I vote for amazing.

"Bye girls," mom says. "Have a great first day at school, be good and tell your Uncle I said 'hi'. Call you later."

"Bye mommy," we say in unison.

Leaving the house, I walk Darlene to the corner to meet my Uncle John. I don't walk or get a ride with Uncle John, I take the school bus with the rest of the kids who are going to Stonywood High School. Stonywood is twenty minutes away from here on Bolton Avenue.

Hope I don't see those rough Williams twins on the bus.

I wait in front of the house to wait with the other kids for bus #17. It's now 7:15. All of the neighborhood kids are walking this way from Eastend Avenue, Southgate Avenue, Westend Avenue, and Northgate Avenue. Some are dragging their feet and they look pretty tired. Others are loud, talkative and excited to see everyone waiting for the bus.

Quieter voices are interrupted by two loud mouths with boisterous body language, bouncing curls, and gum smacking lips. It's the Williams twins: Marvetta and Angelee. The first day of school is just another chance for them to be intimidating and annoying.

"Move outta my way!" Marvetta Williams yells. "We got first dibs on the seats on this bus. Ya'll betta get in back of us."

Great. My worst first day of school nightmare has come true. I refuse to let the twins and their drama ruin my day. I look through my backpack for my schedule and totally avert my attention away from the terror twins.

Yes! I got all of the classes I want. I can't wait. Time for a repeat performance of staying on my 'A' game. I was a good student at Regent-Stanford Middle. Although I encountered the occasional verbally harsh teacher, I usually existed under the radar of teachers who pick on kids who are different because I was always well behaved, completed all of my assignments, and only socialized with the smartest kids in the class. I'm a nerd and I'm proud of it.

Was I a teacher's pet? Uh yeah! I was always the line leader. I didn't have to eat lunch in the cafeteria all the time; I could eat in one of my teacher's room and do my homework. I was always invited to special programs, where teachers only pick the best students to go. I can't forget the time me and five other students were given St. Louis Cardinals baseball tickets for being the top students on the honor roll and for perfect attendance. Who wouldn't want to be a teacher's pet? But I didn't brag about it. Bragging only gets you ostracized from all of the other kids. I still wanted to have friends and be liked.

I know how to get good grades, but I want to be noticed for other things at Stonywood. Other talents than what I showed at Regent-Stanford. There's only so much you can do in middle school. We had the choir, art club and soccer. If you weren't into any of those activities, you weren't showcasing anything.

I can daydream all day about my perfect, ideal social life and classes at Stonywood, but what's a dream without actually living the true reality of it all? My best friend Kevin understands, he's been looking forward to going to Stonywood High for the longest. Kevin's my boy, always has been since third grade. Watching him walk up to the bus stop, he looks older to me. Everyone looks older after the summer break.

"What's up Deanne?" Kevin asks.

"Kevin, is that a moustache I see?" I ask.

"Of course, I'm a man now!" Kevin says.

"Ha ha!" I say. "Looking pretty nice, new clothes I see?"

"You know I had to come fresh with the matching denim and blue polo. Oh new Jordans too."

"Thanks for the fashion report."

"Let me look at you though," Kevin says. He walks around me as if he's checking me out from head to toe. "Not bad, not bad. You might get a boyfriend you keep this up."

"Whatever," I say. "I'm not looking for a boyfriend. So what else is going on?"

"Nothing much," Kevin says. "You know Jason's still having asthma attacks. Had one this morning, scaring my mom and dad half to death. They had to take him to the hospital before school."

"Sorry to hear that," I say. "I hope he gets better."

"Yeah me too," Kevin says.

I hear a yell from behind the line, it's Michelle and Daphne.

"Wait, wait, don't leave yet we're coming!" Everyone boards the bus, and starts to compare class schedules.

"Kevin let me see your schedule so I can see

if we have any classes together," I say.

Kevin opens his schedule and then hands it to me.

"Ah, look," I say. We have Advanced English together."

"That's what's up," Kevin says laughing. "So I'm going to have my own personal tutor, Deanne Summers."

"You must be smoking something, Kev."

"You know I hate writing D. You have got to help me with those trillion page papers homie."

"The only person's work I'm doing is the girl you're staring at. Me."

The bus pulls off. I decide to close my eyes and block out the sound of the Williams twins singing and shouting:

"Southgate, Southgate, we on top!

Southgate, Southgate—we the Queen B's!

Southgate, Southgate—yeah that's me!

Southgate, Southgate—we got it poppin!

Southgate, Southgate—ain't no stopping us!"

If I was the bus driver I would lose it on these kids. Not a job for someone who hates kids. The kids don't care how noisy and disrespectful they are. Just maybe we'll get lucky and the bus driver will kick the Williams twins off the bus.

"You kids settle down and be quiet back there or I'm gonna pull this bus over!"

The bus driver isn't playing.

A few minutes of quiet and then it's right back to the noise. The Williams twins and their friends make more noise than anyone needs to hear this early in the morning. They all know the bus driver isn't going to pull over. He has to get us to school on time.

Kevin, Michelle and Daphne are talking about what they did over the weekend. The Williams twins stop rapping and start arguing with some girl about which of their outfits looked better. Kids are listening to iPods, playing video games and showing off new cell phones.

I'm not interested in any of what's going on. Too busy thinking. And you know what? I love my Southgate Avenue friends, Kevin, Daphne and Michelle, but honestly, sometimes they get on my nerves. They talk about the same old stuff, every time I see them. Who's wearing what. Who they don't want to see at school. What reality TV star got punched in the face for flirting with someone else's boyfriend. I have to find some new friends! But is it really that easy? I've known my Southgate friends for years. There's nothing wrong with branching out though, to learn new things, and talk about new things. First day of high school. Yeah, a new beginning.

ẽẽẽ

CHAPTER 2

PREPPIES, FASHIONISTAS
& JOCKS

After a twenty-five minute scenic drive through University City, bus #17, carrying all of the Southgate Avenue kids, finally arrives at Stonywood High. The school is located on a tree-lined, grassy, well-kept campus consisting of the Main two-floor building and the three-floor Annex. Stonywood was known for its beautiful track and field and rigorous academic regime. The Main building housed classrooms, the main office and counselor's offices. The Annex housed classrooms, the art and dance studios, the gym, student health clinic and auditorium.

Stonywood starts at 9th grade and ends with 12th. The school is in the center of a mixed and diverse community of people: white, black, East Indian and Asians. Beautiful homes with manicured lawns surround it, as well as several parks, a golf course, apartment living for senior citizens, and a strip mall complete with a McDonald's, Payless shoe store, nail salon and Target. Students who live in the neighborhood walk to school, ride a bike, are dropped off by their parents, or bused in. I'm bused in with the rest of the Southgate Avenue kids. Students from all over University City, from the five middle schools come to Stonywood High for a new and challenging social and academic experience.

I can't wait for the bus to come to a stop.

"Stay seated and wait until I get the signal to let you off," the bus driver says.

Each of us look out the windows to view the fifteen to twenty school buses of students arriving and unloading, some already parked in front of bus #17, others were across the street, and the rest drove up the hill from behind.

"Look at all those buses!" Michelle says.

"There must be thousands of kids getting off of them," Daphne says. "Look!"

"It's just middle school times ten," Kevin says. "No big deal to me."

Kevin, Michelle, Daphne, and me, the Southgate

Avenue Crew as we call ourselves, step off the bus and stand around momentarily to give each other unified, unspoken encouragement before we wander off to find our classes.

"Hope you all find your classes before the late bell," I say.

"Yeah, me too," Michelle says.

I see kids walking in pairs and groups, some dropping books in their hands, others steadying their shoulders to carry heavy bags packed to the max with notebooks, pens, clothes for P.E. and lunches.

Call it being nosey but I'm searching their faces to see who's sure of themselves, and who's not. I'm checking out the fashionistas and the jocks. They're always the most popular in high school, so I've heard. I admire the eclectic mix of students walking through the campus, and their styles: the jewelry and dress of an Indian girl, the spunky and colorful look of a punk kid, the crisp and clean look of a group of preppies, the creative look of natural haired black girls, and the hip hop inspired look of a group of Asian kids. And then of course there were the baggy pants, jersey and sweatband wearing black boys, ghetto fabulous, video vixen looking, black girls and the polo and loafer wearing white girls.

"These girls are all out to impress on the first day," Daphne says. "But you know that fades after awhile."

"You can only have so many new clothes in the beginning of the year before everything you have starts to look old," Michelle says.

"Y'all sound so insecure," I say. "What's the matter?" I ask.

"Nothing," Daphne says. "I don't know if I can keep up with the fashion show that is Stonywood."

Michelle and Kevin pretend to be in model poses.

"Y'all can joke me all you want to," Daphne says.

"I wouldn't worry about it Daph," I say. "You always look good."

Most of them are rich anyway," Kevin says. "But they always copy off of kids from the hood. We are the leaders Daphne. Remember that."

"I'm with Kevin on that," I say.

"Deanne," Michelle asks. "Are you down to go to Cicero's after school?"

"Yeah D., you know I'm going to have the 411 on what's going on here," Kevin chimed in. "We definitely need to catch up right after school."

"Fine with me," I say. "I just have to be home by the time Darlene gets there at five. Mom doesn't get home until 6:30pm."

"Sounds like a plan," Kevin says. "Let's meet at the bus. Deanne we're headed the same way to English. Daph,' 'Chelle, catch y'all later."

"Alright, see y'all. Bye," said Daphne and Michelle in unison.

Daphne and Michelle walk away in the opposite direction. Now Kevin and I just have a few minutes to get to our class on time.

"I'm so excited, but I don't want to look too pressed. I really need to calm my nerves," I say.

"Yeah calm down D." Kevin says. "Stop talking and help me find this class in the Main building."

"Alright, let's go."

ଏଏଏ

CHAPTER 3
I KNOW MAYA TOO

Kevin and I move through a sea of students, all herded in the same direction by school administration. Here we are—Advanced English, Room #120 with ten more minutes before class start time.

"I'm not sitting in the front," Kevin says. "You know, all up in the teacher's face."

"You want to sit in the back?" I ask.

"Of course."

"Not me. Only two types of kids sit in the back; those who don't want to do their work, and those who don't know how. I'm neither."

"Ah, second row."

"Fine."

Second row isn't too bad. Close enough to see and hear everything, and far enough that we're not 'all up in the teacher's face' as Kevin put it. Mrs. Cutchens' classroom is pretty normal, as far as English classes go. She has a dozen or so plants hanging or sitting on the window sills. There is an area for independent reading in the back of the room with two comfy chairs, a bean bag, a large multi-colored rug and a mini-library filled with textbooks and novels. On the walls, hang posters bearing covers of popular book titles and images of Zora Neale Hurston, Toni Morrison, Sandra Cisneros, Maya Angelou, Langston Hughes and William Shake-speare.

"Who turned on the heat?" A boy with a short sleeve hoodie and headphones on says.

"Yeah," Kevin says. "It's so hot in here you can see the steam coming off of the heaters."

"Open the windows," a girl says. "I'm sweating and I haven't even had gym yet."

There's only one window cracked. We don't even wait to ask Mrs. Cutchens if she wants the windows open. Next thing you know Kevin and a few other students get up to open all of the windows. The smell of honeysuckle wafts in through the windows from the bushes outside. And now all I want to do is go outside and lay in the sunshine. But I can't class is about to start.

Mrs. Cutchens walks in and stands at the blackboard with her back facing the class. She turns around briefly to see who has just cursed loudly in the room, about the room temperature "finally" being bearable. She cuts her eyes at him when he met her stare. Mrs. Cutchens turns back around to face the board to write her name and date. She rifles through papers and books on her desk, seemingly oblivious to the fact that students are coming in late and several still aren't seated. She grabs a notebook and book from her desk.

Looking around the room I see that the students in the Advanced English class are diverse. The majority of students are white. There are four black kids including me and Kevin, three Asian students and one Indian girl. Seeing my new classmates and teacher, a sense of confidence and pride comes over me. I've always loved reading and writing. This class will probably be like my second home.

Mrs. Cutchens is a brown skinned black woman with reddish brown hair coiffed in a French roll. She wears reddish-brown lipstick and gold hoop earrings dangle from her ears. Mrs. Cutchens' round face had slight creases near the eyes and in her forehead, my mom calls those "worry line." Thick-bodied, she wears a tan button up sweater, a white oxford shirt, dark brown knee-length skirt, matching dark brown pumps, bare legs and a gold ankle bracelet on her left ankle. The simple gold band on her ring finger says she's married. I wonder if she has any children?

Everyone is settled in their seats. Students are opening backpacks to take out notebooks and pens while we wait for Mrs. Cutchens to finish being self-occupied.

"What's up with this lady?" Kevin asks. "She hasn't even bothered to say good-morning to us."

"She's rude," a girl behind Kevin says.

"She's not that excited to be here on the first day," I say. "Or she's just real laid back."

When Mrs. Cutchens finally greets the class, she does it in an unusual way; she recites an excerpt of *I Know Why the Caged Bird Sings* by Maya Angelou. When she's done, Mrs. Cutchens looks pleased with herself. She sits on a stool at the front of the class.

"Can any of you tell me what you know about Maya Angelou?" She asks.

Several students raise their hands. One red-headed

white girl with freckles wearing a yellow polo and denim skirt, in the front row, seems especially giddy about answering. The girl waves her hand back and forth as if Mrs. Cutchens couldn't see her. Mrs. Cutchens overlooks the other six students whose hands are up, including mine. She calls on freckle face.

"Tell us what you know about Maya Angelou," Mrs. Cutchens says. "And tell me your name first."

The girl nods her head repeatedly, anxiously waiting for her chance to talk. The rest of the class all watches her, listening closely, probably to hear if she really knows anything at all about Maya Angelou.

I kinda hope she doesn't know much so that I can "school" the class on the life of Maya Angelou. Am I competitive? Yes.

"Kevin," I say. "If she doesn't get this, the stage is all mine."

"Hi I'm Kristen Levski," freckle face says. "Maya Angelou was an African American woman, born here in St. Louis. She was raised in both St. Louis and Arkansas. She was an internationally known poet, author, playwright, dancer, director and activist. She wrote twelve acclaimed books of poetry and autobiographies. She is best known for her books *I Know Why the Caged Bird Sings* and *Gather Together in My Name*. She has a son named Guy and she's Oprah Winfrey's godmother." Freckle face smiles at Mrs. Cutchens and then turns around to smile at her classmates including me. How creepy. It's just a question, not a pageant.

"Deanne don't be jealous," Kevin says. "This is Advanced English. What—you thought you were the only smarty in the class?"

"Hush Kevin."

Before Mrs. Cutchens could comment, I made sure to raise my hand. There are a few minor details freckles left out.

"Oh Mrs. Cutchens," I say. "She forgot something. Maya Angelou is 'Dr.' Maya Angelou because she received many honorary doctorate degrees. Dr. Angelou was a distinguished college professor and her birth name was Marguerite Johnson."

Sitting taller in my chair now, if I were Lebron, that'd be a slam dunk. Miss Freckles just gave me the side eye. If you can't stand the heat, get out of the kitchen, well I mean the Advanced English class. And this class is now getting hot, literally.

Kevin gives me dap. Mrs. Cutchens gives me a "nice job" look. Whatever. I'm just here to make an 'A' and keep it all year.

"Well both of you are correct," Mrs. Cutchens says.

"Kristen, you seem to know so much about Maya Angelou. Did you study her for a project in middle school?" Mrs. Cutchens asks.

"No, not really," Kristen says. "My mother is an English professor at Washington University. When Maya Angelou visited there to give a talk, my mother took my brother and I along."

Mrs. Cutchens turns toward me.

"And you young lady," she says. "What did you say your name was?"

"Deanne. Deanne Summers."

"Deanne you also seem to know a lot about Dr. Maya Angelou," she says. "Is she one of your favorite writers?"

"Yes, she's one of my favorite poets, besides Sonia Sanchez, June Jordan, Nikki Giovanni and Langston Hughes," I say.

"Great."

"Can I read something for the class?" I ask.

"Sure what is it?" Mrs. Cutchens asks. "The class

doesn't mind, right?

Murmurs, snickers, awkward laughter and yawns could be heard around the room. With a few "No" not at alls, and "go" for its.

"It's a poem I wrote."

"Love to hear it," Mrs. Cutchens says looking interested.

I'm getting out of my seat. Feeling a little nervous but I can't show it. So here it goes. Deanne the poet.

Fresh and lovely
my skin bares no scars
Fearless and defiant
like a man rotting behind bars

My mind is sharp and discerning
so I use it like a weapon
I am precious and brilliant
like diamonds
none are equal in comparison

I can teach you to dance like lighting
or sing of the blues

I am the baddest little sista with no bounds

who knows no common rules

My lyrics are dynamic

my words speak the truth

You can say I'm a poet

carrying a truthful pen like Maya Angelou

"Deanne wow!" Mrs. Cutchens says, "You really wrote that?"

"Yes I did."

Mrs. Cutchens and most of the class, except for a few dumbfounded students including Kristen Levski, claps for me. How nice. Maybe next time I'll get a standing ovation, but I won't count on it.

"This is what I want for my students," Mrs. Cutchens says.

"What does she want?" Kevin says. "For us to all be spoken word poets?"

"Shhh, she's talking." I say.

"I want for you to have a love and passion for literature," Mrs. Cutchens says. "That is why we're all here. Do you agree?

"We all agree we're here to pass this class so we can graduate," Kevin says.

Students laugh.

A girl next to me whispers. "What's the assignment? Too much talking with this lady."

Mrs. Cutchens goes on.

"I want you to have knowledge of great writers, and to explore your own creative expression. We'll do all of these things in my class. Thank you Deanne for that unexpected, yet uplifting poem presentation. I'll be talking to you in the spring about joining my poetry club, you too Kristen, if you girls are interested."

"That would be great Mrs. Cutchens," I say.

"Me too, Mrs. Cutchens," Kristen chimed in. "Count me in."

"So what about lyricists? Rappers?" Kevin asks.

"We'll talk more about that as the semester goes on," Mrs. Cutchens says. "But of course all creative writers are welcome."

Mrs. Cutchens spent the rest of the class time assigning English textbooks for each of us and discussing the first reading selection—Catcher in the Rye.

"Okay, that was the bell," Mrs. Cutchens says. "You're

dismissed. Don't leave any trash, take all of your belongings. Have a good day and see you guys tomorrow."

Kevin and I began to walk out of the class.

"Yo, Deanne I didn't know you could spit poetry like that," Kevin says. "Girl you are baaaaad! When did you write that poem?"

"This summer," I say. "It's just something I get into when I'm alone. I'll probably write more since Mrs. Cutchens is having a poetry club."

I hear someone calling me from behind.

"Hey Deanne, Deanne." It's Kristen.

"Nice job on the poetry," she says. "Maybe we can study together sometime, you know since we're both poetry lovers."

"Oh hey," I say. "I don't usually study with anyone but you know we'll see."

"Why don't we exchange numbers?" Kristen asks.

This girl is pretty aggressive in the friend getting department. Kinda caught me off guard. Kevin gives me an odd look, then moves forward to introduce himself.

"Kristen, what's up? I'm Kevin," he says. "Deanne I'll catch you later, gotta run to science."

I give Kevin a "don't leave me now look," but it's too

late. He gives the peace out sign and walks off in the opposite direction.

"Yeah, I'll see you later. Thanks Kev," I say.

"So what school did you come from?" I ask. Kristen takes paper and pen out of her backpack.

"Glade Park in the Heights."

Glade Park is a school that mostly wealthy white kids go to, and some black kids who are bused in. Located in Terrace Heights, the school has received national awards and is in the most beautiful neighborhood in University City. Beautiful meaning—no trash, big houses and lots of flower gardens.

"Oh yeah, Glade Park, I've heard of it."

"So what school did you come from?" Kristen squints her blue eyes. She's studying me. No problem. I'm studying her too.

"Regent-Stanford. It's an okay school. The ice cream socials were always fun."

"One of my neighbors' father teaches there. Did you know Mr. Clark?" Kristen asks.

"Mr. Clark taught fourth grade. I never had him though."

She's staring at me as if I'm some kind of a unique

animal. Does she want to take me home and dissect me?

I hand Kristen my number. She hasn't written hers down yet. She seems like she's in a daze, preoccupied with her thoughts. But she's still staring at me. What gives?

"You speak really well for a black girl. You're very smart I can tell. I like your style too."

"I speak really well for a black girl?" I ask. "What's that suppose to mean? I don't know whether to feel insulted or complimented. What if I told you, YOU talk really well for a white girl?"

How crazy! I don't even wait for her reply. Later for her. I start to walk off.

"Wait, Deanne! I didn't mean it like that. I was just admiring you that's all. You seem really cool. I meant no disrespect."

I turn around and walk toward her.

"Well I speak really well because that's how I was raised to speak," I say. "I'm no different from most of the kids around here. Look I'm late to class, if you want to catch up later, write your number down quickly."

I'm feeling irritated but I guess she didn't mean anything by it. Kristen scribbles her number in green ink on a polka dotted note pad. I notice her name is inscribed in red cursive letters at the top of each note.

This girl has her own stationary. Deep.

I check out Kristen's style, very preppy: moccasins, denim skirt, yellow Izod polo shirt, Coach leather backpack, and her long bushy red hair was tied up in a neat yellow bow.

Kristen is more posh than Posh Spice. Definitely a rich girl. Kristen hands me her number and it's time to rush to class.

"Call me or I'll call you," she says.

"Cool," I say.

Down the hall I glance at my schedule, and then look for the classroom where my second period Advanced Social Studies class is. I'm still thinking about Kristen.

I'm not too bad in the fashion department, but why does Kristen want to be my friend? What does a girl who seems like she probably has everything want from me? I'm far from rich and I live in a totally different part of the city—not the wealthy part. I guess I'm lucky that mom has always made sure that me and Darlene never go without anything. We're not poor, mom just has to work really hard.

One thing education is like really important to mom. She always reminds us that it can open doors and that our family has always been "educated and dignified from many generations past."

Mom says, "Genius is in your blood Deanne."

When mom talks like that I know she's serious. It's like the weight of black history is on my shoulders for me to succeed.

I came to Stonywood High to make my mark and meet new friends. But does that mean I have to only stick to having black friends?

ℰℰℰ

CHAPTER 4

A HATER AND A TAPPER

Of course I enter Advanced Social Studies late after talking to Kristen so long. My teacher, Mrs. Aioli, a tall woman with short blond hair, doesn't look pleased. Great first impression Deanne.

"Young lady, do you have a late pass? All students are required to have a pass when entering the class late," Mrs. Aioli says in a perturbed tone.

"No, I don't," I say.

My face is burning with embarrassment. I quickly find a seat.

I look around the class for my Southgate Avenue friends Michelle and Daphne, who are sitting in the back row of the class, the far right corner. We all give mini-waves to each other. Mrs. Aioli talks about the history of American government, the class' first unit of study, I take out a pen and notebook to take notes. Mrs. Aioli hands out a class schedule syllabus and discusses the weekly reading assignments, papers and exam schedule.

I glance at Michelle and Daphne and give a funny-faced frown to the both of them. Michelle is looking in her compact mirror while putting on M.A.C. lip gloss. Daphne looks bored to death, her head down staring at the floor. My friends look less than studious right about now. Oh well.

I'm taking copious notes and start feeling an annoying tapping on the back of my chair. Okay third tap, time to turn around and see who this is. I turn around to see a tall, dark eyed, brown haired, white boy tapping nervously, as if he's totally unaware. I give him a glance like, "Uh can you quit it?"

"Oh, sorry," he says in a low voice tone, trying not to interrupt Mrs. Aioli. He stops tapping, momentarily. I'm trying to tune it out but I can't. The tapper is totally breaking my concentration. This time, eye contact won't cut it.

"Would you mind not doing that?" I ask.

"No problem. Sorry. Bored I guess," he says.

What's his problem? I really don't have time to wonder what his problem is for too long. Mrs. Aioli has started going around the room asking each student to introduce themselves and state what school they come from.

Now it's the girl in front of me.

"Mavis Jones," she says. "Munroe Middle." Mavis' pops gum in between each word.

She has attitude. My turn.

"Deanne T. Summers. I attended Stanford-Regent."

Now it's the tapper's turn.

"Palmer Pirro," he says. I'm from Glade Park."

Once all twenty-five students are finished introducing themselves, Mrs. Aioli asks each student to come to her desk and sign for their social studies textbook. I walk past Mavis Jones' desk to get my book. Mavis inconspicuously and purposefully moves her backpack in my way, making me stumble and almost fall before I catch myself.

"Why'd you do that?" I turn to ask Mavis. She gives me a nasty look and rolls her eyes.

"Oops," she says in a dry tone.

I pick up my book from Mrs. Aioli and try to keep calm. Why would anyone want to start beef on the first day of school? Someone who's hating. Mavis has been dismissed in my mind and now branded a hater.

Moments later, the bell sounds ending second period. Michelle and Daphne come over to me to meet me at the door. I grab my stuff, and start walking toward the door. Then I see Mavis walking really, really slow in front of me like she's trying to stall me from getting to the door. Mavis turns around and looks at me. What on earth for?

"Watch it, you almost bumped into me," Mavis says. Mavis rolls her eyes at me so hard, I'm waiting for both to pop right out of their sockets. This girl has got to be nuts.

"No I didn't," I say.

She gives me a hard look and walks out of the door. Michelle and Daphne step toward me.

"No she didn't!" Michelle says. "You want me to go take care of that D.?"

"No, " I say. "We don't need anymore drama. I'm not going to let her get to me. I have too much to focus on."

"Well maybe you're right," Daphne says. "Who wants to get into a fight on the first day? So ghetto. That girl Mavis has a problem y'all."

"Bye Mrs. Aioli," I say. "See you tomorrow."

I walk out with Michelle and Daphne. Hope I don't run into boogerface Mavis again.

"Hey, Deanne."

I stop and turn to see Palmer Pirro, the tapper.

"What does he want?" Daphne asks.

"What's up?" I ask.

"I'm sorry again about tapping on your chair. I got a little bored. Social studies has never been my favorite subject. So you went to Regent-Stanford?"

"Yup," I say.

"Well did you know Mrs. Pirro, the art teacher over there?"

"Sure did. I was in her class in 7th grade."

"She's my mom. Jennifer Pirro."

"Really? She was a really nice lady, one of my favorite teachers. We always did a lot of fun projects with her. I remember when she took us on a field trip to the St. Louis Art Museum."

"She's cool. You know for a mom who's a teacher."

We both laugh. I hear what he's saying. It would be kind of weird if my mom taught at my school. Even though I love her, I like having a break to just see my friends during the day.

"So what class do you have next?" Palmer asks.

"Deanne, we gotta go," Michelle says.

"We'll catch you after school right? Daphne asks.

"Okay, see you all later then," I say.

Michelle and Daphne walk off giggling, looking behind their shoulders at me and Palmer.

"Oh, I have physical science next with Diamond," I say.

"Me too. I'll walk with you."

❧

One minute before the bell rings. Science class is pretty crowded. Mr. Diamond has already started to call the attendance. I'm sitting near an open window. It's just too hot in here. Palmer sits down right next me. It's the first day and he has a fan club already. A few girls from the back of the room call his name. "Hiiiii Palmer." It's so annoying when girls draw out "Hi." They sound so desperate to be noticed.

Physical science is going to be a hot mess, literally. It's hot and crowded and Mr. Diamond seems amused with himself as he cracks jokes while giving us his lecture. He's totally oblivious to all of the flirting and chatter going on in class.

After physical science I meet Kevin for lunch.

The lunchroom is like any other school lunch room, filling with some good and some bad food smells. Today's lunch: cheese or pepperoni pizza, salad, french fries and an assortment of cookies and puddings. I'm going for cheese pizza, a salad and a Sprite.

I see Kevin and we both grab a table.

"Deanne check this out," Kevin says. "I got a new watch, fresh diamonds in it and everything. What you know about that, huh? Check it out."

Kevin turns rolls his wrist back and forth.

"Kevin, where did you get something like that?" I ask. "You don't have a job."

"You know my boy Damon let me hold onto it for awhile," he says. "He has so much fresh gear, he let me borrow it. You know your boy Kev' has to stay fresh girl."

"Yeah okay," I say. I give Kevin my shadiest side eye look possible, letting him know what I really think. One of Kevin's friends sits down at the table before I can further inspect the shady watch.

"What's up Kev?" You shootin' ball with us or what?"

"Hey Jahmir," Kevin says. "You know it man. I'll meet y'all out there on the court after while. Gotta few runs to make first though."

Kevin and Jahmir give each other dap. Jahmir looks over at me.

"And who is this?" he asks.

"This is Deanne my homegirl from Southgate. D. this is Jahmir Johnston. He went to Riverview last year."

"Hey."

Jahmir's not bad looking. His skin is a beautiful honey color. His dark eyes have the longest eye lashes I've ever seen on a boy. His hair is cut real close. And he smells good. White Polo, baggy jeans, clean white Jordans. But then he opens his mouth, and all I see are "grillz". Gold front teeth. Gleaming. One large diamond earring in left ear and a gold link chain around his neck. Baller. Definitely not my type.

"Yeah I just transferred in as a junior. You a freshman?"

"Yup."

"So how you like Stonywood so far?"

"It's cool."

"How do you like Stonywoood?"

"It's chill. I'm just trying to stay outta trouble and make the basketball team so it's all good."

Jahmir gets up from the table.

"Alright Kev, check you later."

"Alright J."

"Deanne, stay sweet. Maybe I'll see you around."

"Maybe," I say.

Some kind of player. Too much of a baller for me. My pizza is getting cold and with only a few minutes left for lunch, time to scarf it down along with my salad.

"Yo, I think Jahmir likes you D.," Kevin says.

"Whatever," I say. "He's a player, you can tell by all of that jewelry he wears."

"Naw he's cool," Kevin says.

"I'm heading to class Kev," I say. "I'll see you later."

Okay I'm not going to lie. Jahmir left an impression on me, but I don't know if it's a good one. He gave me this strange feeling in the pit of my stomach, it's like the feeling you get before you go on a roller coaster ride at Six Flags. It's a feeling that's halfway between motion sickness and excitement. What is that? No boy ever looked at me like that before. Jahmir is too flashy. Not my type. At all.

ℰ ℰ ℰ

Chapter 5
Cicero's

The day flies by. The P.E. teacher made us run on a timer. Math is the usual mind boggler, but at least we get to use calculators. Spanish is exciting since this is my third year taking it. Library skills was cool because I love reading and doing research.

It's finally 2:30 and I'm relieved. Everyone I met today made it fun or interesting to say the least. Well not Mavis, she can kick rocks. But everyone else I think is okay, like Kristen and Palmer and maybe even Jahmir. Palmer is like the guy all the girls want because he's just an all American boy. And Jahmir, he's kinda mysterious. Maybe I'm stereotyping and there's more to both of them than I could possibly know right now. Right? Either way, I'm doing what I set out to do, which is meet new people. Jahmir cute—but flashy. Palmer nice—but dorky. That's my assessment. After the bus ride back to Southgate Avenue, I catch up with Kevin, Michelle, and Daphne for pizza at Cicero's.

Kevin is the first one to start talking.

"What's up with your girl Kristen, Deanne?" She was straight up pressed to talk to you after class."

A string of mozzarella pizza hangs out of his mouth from the slice of Sicilian.

"She's cool," I say. "She wants a study partner."

I sprinkle garlic and oregano on my pepperoni slice.

"Yeah, right. She just wants you to hook her up with one of your homeboys," says Michelle.

Michelle sips on her Pepsi and slaps five with Daphne.

"You guys are so wrong. She doesn't really seem like she's into the homies," I say.

"Well what do the two of you have in common anyway?" You live on Southgate Avenue and she probably lives in the Heights. You don't know her," Michelle says rolling her eyes.

"Oh and what about Peter? What was up with him, the dude from social studies?" Daphne asks.

"His name is Palmer, not Peter. Would you all just chill out? There's nothing wrong with meeting new people on the first day. Kristen was friendly toward me and so was Palmer."

Now I'm defensive. Kevin, Michelle and Daphne are grilling me about everyone I met. I'm sure they met some new people too. What's the deal?

"Anyway before y'all start a cat fight up in here let me tell you about my day. These girls in my math class kept hawkin' a brother, you know they like my style," Kevin says.

Daphne throws a balled up napkin at Kevin.

"Whatever Kevin. Make sure you hit the books before you mack the girls," I say.

"Yeah Kevin. It's not cute to be failing before the semester even starts. We know how you are!" Michelle says.

We all laugh at Kevin's expense as he pretends to pose like a model, popping his collar and raising an eyebrow.

The pizza slices are gone. We continue to talk about the first day at Stonywood. The teachers. The cool students and the weird ones. And which classes are going to be hard. No one brings up Mavis. I don't either.

After two hours passed, time to head home.

"Alright guys, I'm out."

"Alright D."

Everyone says good bye. Kevin walks me home. Michelle and Daphne are stopping at the drugstore before they head home. Time to meet Darlene. Thinking about all of my friends questions, makes me think again about Kristen and Palmer. What do I have in common with them? I'm sure I'll find out.

ಌಌಌ

CHAPTER 6

S - P - I - R - I - T

After the first four weeks I've pretty much grown used to my routine at Stonywood. Michelle, Daphne and Kevin have too. Now it's time for me to get involve with after school activities and sports. Stonywood is known for its talented football and basketball teams. The school is basically divided into those who play sports, those who cheer the sports, those who could care less about the sports and those who envy the athletes.

Stonywood also has track, soccer, and lacrosse; sports that although aren't considered as exciting as football or basketball, are still well supported by students, faculty and parents. I'm not a jock but I can cheer the sports and support my school.

Michelle, Daphne and I see a flyer hanging near the door on our way out of social studies.

"Deanne look. There's a flyer about stuff you can

sign-up to try out for. Look there's cheerleading, School Spirit Committees, student government and the dance company. Anything look interesting to you?" Michelle asks.

"Yeah. School Spirit, dance or both. You know we're taking dance together in the spring. Should be fun."

"The teachers who head the activities will be at all the lunches. We should check it out," Michelle says.

"Well count me out. The only thing I want to do is schoolwork and boy scoping," Daphne says.

Daphne and Michelle give each other dap.

"You go right ahead and scope the boys while I make a 4.0 average." I say.

"Girl go on with your bad self," Michelle says. "We'll be right along with you, at least somewhere between a 2.5 and 3.0."

It's hard not to tee hee at that one, but I know Michelle is speaking the truth. Those two are not the most focused when it comes to school.

∾

Later I head to lunch ready to find the tables for the freshman School Spirit Committee and school dance company. The School Spirit Committee table is decorated with streamers and balloons of the school's colors, purple and gold. Two upperclassmen wearing name tags are sitting at the table.

Tiffany Hess is black with long, sleek hair, perfectly cut bangs, a French manicure, dainty pearl earrings, a pretty white button-up blouse, jeans and red pumps on. Sara Boyd is a brunette with big green eyes, plenty of black eye make-up on, wearing a fitted black short-sleeve knit top, black slacks and black boots. She has tattoos. She's very goth.

"Hi. Are you interested in joining a School Spirit Committee?" Sara asks.

"Yes," I say.

"Great," Sara says.

"What year are you?" Tiffany asks.

"A freshman," I say.

"Fresh meat!" Sara says.

"Sara and I are both seniors," Tiffany says. "We're on our way out so it's good to have the underclassmen who will carry the torch in the years to come."

"Here," Sara says. "Fill out this form on our clipboard so we can keep in touch and inform you of our first meeting. We never do the first couple of games, students really need to focus on their work in the first month."

"Here's a little bit about school spirit," Tiffany says. "We sit in the lower stands and hype up the games by chanting, singing songs, doing quirky dances, holding up signs and twirling party favors. You know anything fun to bring school spirit to the people in the stands and make the players feel good. We occasionally get water for the cheerleaders and anyone else down in that area, who might need something."

"One more thing," Sara says. "We design, print and post flyers and announcements for upcoming games, and school parties. We also organize the end of the year Stonywood Annual Barbecue at Herman Park. Does all of this sound like something you want to get involved with?"

"Totally. I love doing stuff like that! It sounds like a lot of fun."

"It's fun," Tiffany says. "But it's also a lot of work. So you have to be able to balance schoolwork and your activities. Things can get pretty crazy."

Sounds like it's going to be perfect for me. Sara and Tiffany are both really cool. I feel a sisterly kinship with Tiffany though. Not just because she's black though. She has the kind of poise, confidence and classy style that I really look up to. Tiffany isn't shrinking in the presence of Sara or acting a clown to get attention. Another thing, Tiffany speaks like a young leader.

I don't have a real life big sister because I'm the big sister. Maybe Tiffany can be my big sister? No, that's thinking too far ahead. She might not have any interest in being a big sister. I don't need to ride on anyone's coat tails. I just want good friends. Really cool friends who I can relate to. I feel guilty for feeling so needy. But what do you do when you meet someone so cool—you just want to adopt them as a sister or something? That's how I feel about Tiffany.

I finish filling out the form and then give it back to Tiffany.

"Here you go," I say. "Let me know when the first meeting is."

"Thanks for stopping by Deanne," Tiffany says. "We'll talk to you soon. Bye."

"Bye Deanne, thanks," Sara says.

"Okay, bye."

Now I have to find the table for the dance company, Absolute Rhythms.

Ugh there it is. There's such a long line. I can't tell if there's a teacher or students behind the table because it's so crowded. Several students clear out and I finally get to the front of the line.

"Next, step up," a petite woman with a black long sleeve leotard and flouncy, purple, wrap skirt says.

"I want to sign-up to be in Absolute Rhythms," I say.

"There's no signing up," she says. "We have auditions this Friday. You'll have to take a 1 1/2-hour class with me and my senior assistant Deandre on Thursday at 3pm, during which time you'll learn a routine and perform it for the audition on Friday. If you can keep up and I like what I see, you'll be asked to be a member. We only have ten slots open, because we already have fifteen who are returning upperclassmen. Oh, by the way I'm Ms. Moshe."

"Great thanks," I say.

"What is your name?" She asks. "You're a freshman?"

"Yes," I say. "My name is Deanne Summers."

"We'll see you on Thursday at 3pm Deanne," she says. "Dance studio in the Annex."

"Okay, see you then," I say.

It's taking everything for me not to skip away like a

five year old. Yes dance auditions! I've been in Saturday dance training since I was six. I'm so ready for this.

I'm officially on a natural high. Now I have two extracurricular activities I know I'll be good at. I'll be more than just another freshman walking around Stonywood. The dance audition should be a piece of cake, but I can already tell Ms. Moshe is nothing to play with. I've been taking ballet, jazz and Dunham technique for years. Dance is one thing I'm always confident about, besides academics.

Mom puts the money aside every month for me and Darlene's classes at Evening Star Dance Academy. Sometimes I take dance classes at the nearby community center on Sunday afternoons. Early in the morning when my mom and Darlene are still sleeping, I go down to the living room, turn on some classical or jazz music to stretch and practice my leaps, arm and leg extensions.

It may sound corny but in my mind, I'm a serious artist in training. I didn't always know what I was training for until now.

ℰℰℰ

CHAPTER 7
SMOKE AND MIRRORS

It's the end of the day and I promised Kristen we would meet in front of the Annex building. She called me last night to ask if I could come to her house and study with her for a couple of hours today. I asked mom if I could go, she was cool as long I left Kristen's number, address and parent's names. My mom is a stickler for that kind of stuff. Safety first. She's a concerned mom. My uncle will have to keep Darlene until I get home a little later.

"Hey Deanne," Kristen says. "How was your day?"

"Great," I say. "Finally figured out what I want to do as far as after school activities. What about your day?"

"It was fine," she says. "Hey you'll have to meet my friends Carly, Abigail, Jessica, Roman, Phillip, Palmer and Andrew. Maybe tomorrow."

"Boy you sure have a lot of friends," I say. "Did you

just meet these people?"

"Course not," she says. "I've known them since kindergarten. We all went to Glade Park together. Our parents know each other and we're neighbors in Mulberry Heights."

"Yeah, sure I'll meet them."

We wait for Kristen's mother to pick us up. Kristen calls her mother on her cell phone.

"Mom, where are you?" She asks. "My friend Deanne is with me. She's coming home with me to study. Can you pick up McDonald's for us? I'm so hungry. Yeah, yeah of course I ate lunch but that doesn't mean anything! Mom, please come on, it won't take you that long to go through the drive through. Okay, good. So how long? When will you be here? Okay, leave work now. Now, mom!"

Wow. I think I would expect a hand to come right through my cell phone to smack me if I ever talked to my mom like that!

Kristen's mom must be a pushover. I guess that's just how they communicate. Thirty minutes later, Kristen's mom pulls up in a white Cadillac Escalade with classical music playing. Red haired and petite with a navy blue suit on and matching heels, Kristen's mom gets out of the car to help Kristen with her bags—a gym bag and her Coach bag.

"Hello," she says. "I'm Mrs. Levski. You must be Deanne?"

She extends her hand to shake mine. Very business-like.

"Hi Mrs. Levski," I say.

We get into the car, and fasten our seatbelts.

"Kristen here you are," Mrs. Levski says. "The McDonald's you wanted. Deanne, Kristen told me about you. I hear you love poetry. That's absolutely wonderful. A lifelong reader makes for a lifelong learner."

I like the way Mrs. Levski talks. Her voice kind of flutters.

"Mom," Kristen whines. "Don't start lecturing. We've heard it all day, now that's enough."

"Oh, it's okay," I say. "Thank you Mrs. Levski. Yes I love poetry. I love to read. My mother has always kept a lot of books in the house for my sister and I."

"How wonderful," Mrs. Levski says. "Well I've done the same with my kids. I teach English at Washington University and poetry is one of the things we focus on. I'll be sure to give Kristen some books I think you might like. The English department receives all sorts of newly released books for free—short stories, poetry collections, novels, you name it."

"That would be great," I say. "I'd like that thank you."

We arrive at Kristen's house. I'm seriously trying to keep my mouth from hanging wide open. The Levski house is a beautiful four-story French style home, complete with sprawling front and back yards, a circular driveway, a three-car garage, and plenty of trees surrounding it "so the neighbors can't see inside," Mrs. Levski says.

There is a pool with a guest-house and patio for barbecuing, in the back of the house.

"Okay girls," Mrs. Levski says. "I have to get to a meeting, but you can call me if anything. Deanne nice meeting you."

"Nice meeting you," I say.

Kristen's mother waves good-bye and drives off.

When we get inside the house, Kristen lazily drops her bags including her half eaten bag of McDonald's on the floor.

"Don't worry, the maid will get it," she says.

And she does. Shirley, the Levski's housekeeper approaches us at the door. "Afternoon girls," Shirley says. She grabs all of the bags.

"Hey Shirley," Kristen says. "This is my friend Deanne, she's going to be studying with me for awhile."

"How you doing?" Shirley asks.

"Good, thank you," I say. Very nice lady. I wonder how she puts up with Kristen's snotty behavior everyday? Oh well maybe she doesn't really notice it.

Kristen doesn't give me a full tour, but I can see from where I'm standing that the house is clean, huge and decorated to the max. There are two living rooms, a dining room, an enormous eat-in kitchen, a pathway leading to the outside deck and patio in the backyard, a laundry room and a guest bedroom and bath on the first floor. The Levski house could definitely rival any celebrity home featured on MTV Cribs.

I follow Kristen into the kitchen. Kristen grabs two glasses from a cabinet and opens the refrigerator.

"Ice tea?" Kristen asks.

"Sure," I say. "What does your father do Kristen?"

"He's a banker," she replies.

"Oh," I say. Makes sense.

After filling two glasses with ice tea and lemon slices
we head upstairs to Kristen's room. Kristen's room is
decorated in Laura Ashley patterns of yellow, gold
and orange floral theme. Her wallpaper, carpet, chairs,
dresser and hamper set all matched her bedding. Kristen's bedroom décor was very feminine and bright. The
bright colors make me feel happy. The room is pretty
comfortable.

"Have a seat," Kristen says. "I'll be back."

I want to be nosey and get up to look around at all
of Kristen's stuff. Like me, she has a lot of stuff. Framed
photographs and artwork on the walls. Lots of clothes
and shoes. Hats. She has a walk in closet. Three book-
shelves filed with books, a desktop computer, an iPad,
a desk and two chairs. Bean bags. Stuffed animals and
dolls on chairs and a small loveseat. It's a lot to take in.

I take out my homework and look at what needs to
be done first. Definitely English.

Kristen comes back, surprisingly with a pack of cig-
arettes and a lighter.

"Raise the window over there for me and hand me
that air freshener," Kristen says. "You want one?"

I shake my head "No."

Kristen hurriedly places a towel under her bedroom door.

"I do this so they won't smell anything now or later."

She giggles and gestures for me to take an unlit cigarette.

"No thanks. I don't smoke."

I started to say, "Not now or ever." But I know that would sound really judgmental. My mom says smoking is one of the deadliest habits around. Not to mention those scary commercials where the smoker says they only have one lung and they're on a breathing tube because they couldn't give smoking up. I don't know any kids who smoke. Kristen's the only one.

"It's no big deal," she says. "I've been smoking since middle school. I steal these from my dad every now and again. He smokes when he's stressed out."

"What do you like about smoking?"

"I like the taste of it and the feel of the smoke going in and out of my body."

Huh? What is she saying? The feel of the smoke going in and out of her body? That sounds like a drug addiction.

Sorry I can't relate.

"We need to start reading *Catcher in the Rye* and get some of the critical analysis questions done," I say.

"Okay let me get the stuff out of my bag." My book and notebook are out. I'm just waiting on Kristen. She's looking around for her notes. The smoke is bothering me. Honestly my mind is starting to wander off.

I wave at the cigarette smoke, trying to push it away from me like I'm swatting at flies.

"Okay ready," Kristen says.

I start reading Catcher in the Rye aloud and for the next hour and a half, we're as focused as any students of advanced English could be. We talk about the chapters and pretty much finish all of the analysis questions.

"Good study session," I say.

"Yeah, pretty good," Kristen says.

Kristen's mom gives me a ride home.

I get in and heat up some dinner mom made. Baked chicken, rice and broccoli. I finish my math homework and head upstairs. Mom is already in bed, probably dozed off with the TV on. Darlene is asleep.

I want to do something I haven't done in awhile—write in my diary. I keep my diary is an old cigar box my grandfather gave me. I hide it under my bed.

Dear Diary,

I'm officially in high school. And it's everything I expected. Stonywood is so over crowded. It's no wonder anyone is able to find their classes. I've been doing really good. Kevin, Michelle and Daphne are still their usual selves, I haven't been hanging with them lately. Surprised? Don't be, I'm doing my thing now.

I have a few new friends. Well I mainly have one new friend. Anyway her name is Kristen Levski. She's white and has long red hair. She's kinda talkative but she's also really smart. Oh and one other little thing: she's rich. Her parents have this huge house in the Heights. She has a brother too. Kristen's really nice, not bitchy and mean like some of the other girls at Stonywood. I just found out Kristen smokes. It was a little weird because she asked me if I wanted a cigarette. I told her no, in a nice way. Kristen probably gets away with it because it seems like her parents are never home. She's spoiled too. I thought I was a princess! I have nothing on Kristen. Everything she wears are top-notch name brands. She'll probably be one of those kids who gets a brand new car right before her sixteenth birthday. I wish my mom could afford those things. But then Kristen has two parents who work. I only have one. As long as she takes me along for the ride in her new car, I'm cool with that! Enough about Kristen.

I'm auditioning to be a member of the dance company at school! It's called Absolute Rhythms and the dance teacher Ms. Moshe is all of that. She's this petite little dance teacher. She's just like Debbie Allen my dance idol. Oh, okay about boys—there's this kid named Palmer in my social studies class. He talks to me a lot. Kinda geeky but nice. English is my favorite subject since I get to write and read everyday. I like P.E. too, but my teacher is a total drill sergeant. She takes Phys. Ed. way too seriously. Hhhhm let's see what else? Oh I'm still going to my Saturday dance classes, gotta stay on top of things. Guess I'll go to sleep now, been a long week. Toodles, D.

ẽ ẽ ẽ

CHAPTER 8

DIFFERENT STROKES,
DIFFERENT FOLKS

I woke up a little late this morning, 6:45am to be exact. Darlene is already up, making toast, hot chocolate and eggs.

"Deanne you want some toast and eggs?" Darlene yells from the kitchen.

"Mmm Hmm," I say.

It's Thursday morning and I have butterflies in my stomach just thinking about the dance audition with Ms. Moshe to be a member of Stonywood's Absolute Rhythms Dance Company.

I took two dance classes back to back last Saturday: jazz and ballet. I'm confident that at least I won't make a fool of myself in front of Ms. Moshe and the other dancers. I finish my wheat toast and eggs. Chase it with a glass of orange juice. I go back upstairs to pick out my clothes for the day and pin up my hair. Shower time and I'm running out of time to get ready as quickly as possible.

Easy grooming. Palmer's cocoa butter lotion, Secret deodorant and my smell good potion for the day—jasmine scented body spray. Curl my ends with my curler and spray a little sheen. Now for my clothes—a green pair of Tommy Hilfiger jeans, and an ivory and green stripped Gap v-neck sweater. Now my brown ankle boots.

I wear silver stud earrings with a matching silver bracelet my mom gave me on my last birthday. I pack a white long sleeve leotard, dance tights and jazz shoes in a pink and purple Danskin bag for my master class with Ms. Moshe.

I check to make sure Darlene is fully dressed. I turn off all of the lights and appliances in the house, lock up and walk out of the house with Darlene. We see our uncle, and I say goodbye to Darlene and my uncle as she gets into the car.

Now waiting for bus #17 with the other Southgate Avenue kids.

"Deanne, what's the deal?" Kevin asks. "Where were

you yesterday? We were looking for you."

"I went to Kristen's to study," I say.

"Yeah? Where does she live?" Michelle asks.

"The Heights."

"The Heights?" Daphne asks. "Her family's raking in that dough huh?"

"Her mom teaches at Wash. U. Her dad works for a bank I guess."

"Did you get to meet her parents? Are they real stuck-up?" Kevin asks.

"I met Kristen's mom," I say. "She's real nice. She bought McDonald's for us and talked to me about poetry."

"So what did you all do the whole time? Talk about boys?" Michelle asks.

"No," I say. "We went to Kristen's room and started reading *Catcher in the Rye* for English."

"I heard those cribs in the Heights are pretty tight," Daphne says. "Did she give you a tour?"

"No, it wasn't even like that," I say. "It's a nice house, but I didn't want to be like, 'Yo, Kristen your crib is phat, show me around!' That's so ghetto and not me."

"Hhhm mmmm," Kevin says. "She sure seems to dig you. Maybe you're on your way to being adopted like on

Different Strokes!"

Kevin slaps five with Michelle and Daphne.

"You're dumb. I have a family. I'm not trying to get adopted by the Levskis."

I playfully punch Kevin on his shoulder. It's all just jokes but in a way I can tell Kevin is not really cool with me being friends with Kristen. He just isn't really saying it.

"So, 'Chelle what's up?" I ask. "Are you and Daphne going to next week's home game?"

"Yeah, thinking about it," she says. "That's if my mother gives me money to buy a new outfit. I heard Stonywood football games are a fashion show. I might be a freshman, but I'm trying to be the baddest freshman female out there!"

"Well I signed up to be on the freshman Spirit Committee," I say. "I'll be out there cheering with signs and flyers and stuff."

"You can always go with us D. It should be fun," Michelle says.

"I know thanks 'Chelle."

❧

When the bus arrives at Stonywood, we all go our

separate ways to class, except for me and Kevin.

"Kevin did you read any of *Catcher in the Rye* last night?"

"I read the first fifteen pages before I fell asleep, it was boring."

"You're kidding? I love it! Holden Caulfield has problems, that's why I like it. Well just think of it this way, read it and ask plenty of questions in class so Mrs. Cutchens can see you're taking an interest even if you don't understand."

"D. You're right. But you know the kid didn't get registered into advanced English without already having some skills."

"Don't ask me for help if you don't read Kev!"

"No doubt."

ℰℰℰ

CHAPTER 9
MASTER CLASS

I've been waiting all day for this. I almost couldn't focus in any of my classes from thinking about the master class with Ms. Moshe, and the Absolute Rhythms audition on Friday.

After changing into my dance gear, I sign my name on a sheet taped to a table in the studio. Students have already started doing warm ups. I find a spot on the floor to stretch my body and warm up. Ms. Moshe comes in with her assistant, Deandre and two African drummers.

"Everyone move to the barres and we're going to place you in height order for warm up," Ms. Moshe says.

The African drummers begin to play. This reminds me of the Katherine Dunham technique class I take in East St. Louis at SIUE. The sounds of the drums are calming and make me want to dance.

After thirty minutes of intense stretching, sit-ups,

push-ups, neck and head rolls, shoulder hunching, toe pointing, foot flexing and back bending, Ms. Moshe divides the class into sets of four to imitate Ms. Moshe and Deandre's dance movements across the floor. Group by group as Ms. Moshe counted, "1, 2, 3, 4...", we kick, glide, contract, bend and curl our bodies. Ms. Moshe combines modern, jazz, and African dance movements for us to carry out across the floor.

I make sure to make my arm and leg extensions sharp. I know they're watching me. They're watching everyone and if you can't keep up, you'll be cut.

I keep my back straight when I need to and my eye on a special point on the wall in front of me so I don't become dizzy. Ms. Moshe and Deandre approach some of the dancers throughout the master class to model a dance they aren't doing correctly. Ms. Moshe nods to me that I'm on the right track. Cool! I'm just going to pretend to be a gazelle or a peacock moving gracefully across the floor. The music carries me.

I can't pay any attention to the competition. A few students have already walked out because the routines Ms. Moshe put together are probably too rigorous for them.

"Students, gather around," Ms. Moshe says. "Time to show you the routine for Friday's official audition for Absolute Rhythm. Everyone move off of the floor to the side and watch."

There are specific elements of the dance I've seen before in my Saturday jazz class. Other parts of the dance are more abstract but not too challenging to learn. Ms. Moshe keeps doing the movements over an over: two fan kicks, two piqué turns to the right and two piqué turns to the left, a dramatic turn then a graceful fall to the floor face down, three rolls then a kick while on the floor to the left and same thing to the right. A crawl toward the standing position, run-run-leap jump, contraction of the back, two pivots, kick-ball-chain, kick-ball-chain, then there were several more movements.

I study Ms. Moshe's facial expressions and the way her petite yet muscular body seems to easily morph from one movement to the next.

"Anyone want to rehearse with me for a few minutes?" Ms. Moshe asks.

I raise my hand and rush to the front, along with several other students. The African drummers play as we shadow Ms. Moshe. We study the movements and fall into line as if we are each others' shadows.

One by one, students leave the center of the floor to grab their bags and leave. I'm the only one left, still shadowing Ms. Moshe. I don't care about staying later than everyone else, I have to master this. Ms. Moshe turns around and sees that I'm the only one here.

"You're still here after everyone has left?" Ms. Moshe asks.

"I got lost in the music and the movements."

"Well I suppose you did," she says. "Think you'll be ready for tomorrow?"

"Yes, I will."

"Good. Make sure you practice at home and we'll see you at 3pm sharp on Friday, ready for the audition."

"See you then. Bye Ms. Moshe."

I'm sweaty and a little sore, but it was worth it. Time to wash up and change. I'm meeting Kristen and her friends at McDonald's.

☙☙☙

CHAPTER 10
J TO THE K

I hear music blaring and Lil Wayne's "How to Love" coming through the speakers. Walking to McDonald's and a shiny black Ford Explorer pulls up alongside of me. Who is this?

He rolls down the passenger side window. It's Jahmir.

"Yo what's up Deanne?"

I almost don't recognize him. He looks so much older sitting in this car. There's five other young men in the car with him. Smoke and a sweet smell is coming out of the car. The smell of strawberry air freshener mixed with the smoke smell. It's making me want to cover my nose. It's not cigarette smoke.

I really want to run, but there's something holding me. I'm curious about what he has to say.

"Hey Jahmir."

"This is my brother Smoke. Back there is my cousins

Kimmey, Todd and Ray. Y'all this is Deanne, she goes to Stonywood."

Jahmir looks me up and down, studying me. "Hey" they all said in unison.

This is awkward. There's something dangerous about Jahmir. He seems older than he is. But he's kinda cute.

"Deanne you looking real good girl," Jahmir says. "Can we give you a ride somewhere? We going to White Castle, you want to go with us? I'll buy you some double cheeseburgers."

He smiles and lets out a lazy laugh. His gold teeth gleam when the sunlight hits.

"No thanks. I'm on my way somewhere."

"You sure? There's room in the back seat?"

"Yeah, room back here shorty," Todd says.

"I'm good," I say.

"Alright then D., I'll see you around," Jahmir says.

I walk off. The car speeds away. I can still here "How to Love."

I probably won't see him around. Stonywood is huge.

℮ ℮ ℮

CHAPTER 11
GOSSIP GIRLS AND BOYS

Kristen and her friends have already ordered at Mickey D's. After the master class I'm pretty hungry.

"Hey, Deanne," Kristen says. "I bought a chicken sandwich for you with a small Sprite and small fries. Is that okay?"

"Thanks Kristen."

"Hey this is Deanne," Kristen says. "My friend from Advanced English. Deanne, this is Carly, Abigail, Jessica, Roman, Phillip, Palmer and Andrew."

"Hey Deanne."

"I know Deanne," Palmer says. "She's in my social studies and science classes. How's it going Deanne?"

"Pretty good. I just took a dance class with Ms. Moshe."

I realize I must sound geeked out about the dance class. I dip a few fries in ketchup and bite on them slowly.

"That's cool," Carly says. "I always wondered what it'd be like to take dance seriously. I've been taking ballet off and on since I was four."

"You should've come to the class today," I say.

"I heard about it," she says. "I guess I'm not all that serious about joining anything this year. Good luck with it, hope you make it."

"Deanne that's great," Kristen says. "If you make it we can come see you in the dance concerts."

"That would be nice."

They all chime in on gossip about who is dating who. Who got caught smoking in the bathroom. Who was caught cheating on a test and who wrecked their mother or father's $50,000 wheels the weekend before, without having a driver's license.

"I'm ready for a party soon," Kristen says. "Who's up for having a Christmas or New Year's Eve party during the break?"

"Ah, you are my dear," Andrew says. "My parents certainly aren't having it. Not after the end of the year bash I threw last year. My parents had to get a new couch from all the food and beverage stains!"

"Well it wasn't me," Abigail says. "Besides your

surgeon parents have enough money to buy a hundred of those couches."

"I say it's time for Kristen to step it up and give us a party," Phillip says. "When was the last time Kris? 7th grade?"

"Oh right," Kristen says. "My parents will be out of town for New Year's Eve, but my brother will be home from Duke, so maybe they'll let me have a little something if I promise to keep it 'spiffy clean', or promise that Shirley will keep it clean."

Everyone's laughing, but it sounds like these house parties can really be a big headache. Kristen smokes, I'm sure some of the rest do too. And they might even drink alcohol. No telling what pent up, rich kids on a break from school will do when their parents aren't home.

I don't really have much to say so I just listen. Getting to know this group is interesting. They're all very smart, but also snotty with the things they say. Maybe I shouldn't judge. They're just being themselves I guess.

Palmer's always nice to me. He seems pretty popular. I wonder why he doesn't have a girlfriend?

They're still fixated on having a party.

"You know what game we gotta play?" Abigail asks.

"What?" Kristen asks.

"Spin the bottle!"

Abigail turns and kisses Palmer on the lips. Surprise.

"Watch it girl!" Palmer says.

"Abigail, your such a flirt!" Kristen says.

This group is crazy. I guess Abigail likes Palmer and that's her way of showing it. I wonder how Palmer feels about the kiss?

ℰ ℰ ℰ

CHAPTER 12
SURPRISE WINK

English class starts with assignment checks with Mrs. Cutchens. Deanne was eager to share what she had.

"Good morning," Mrs. Cutchens says. "Today I need to collect your responses to *Catcher in the Rye* by J.D. Salinger. Pass up your papers to the front."

"Oh snap, D.," Kevin says. "I didn't do mine. Let me peep yours so I can copy."

Kevin is so shady and predictable. I knew having the same class meant he would try and use me as his personal do-my-work-for-me-person.

"Kevin, no," I say.

I'm so annoyed. Kevin couldn't be busier than me or any other student in this class. Why can't he get his homework done? Time to turn into Ms. Not My Problem.

"D. look," he says. "I couldn't do it. I've been hanging out with Damon and his crew, getting in late. I didn't have time to do it."

"Damon and his crew?" I ask. Aren't they drug dealers Kev?"

"Oh come on D.," he says. "That's a rumor. You know Dame's family owns a couple of laundry mats and the wing place over on Page. Anyway, you gonna let me get the paper or what?"

"Kevin, you're slipping," I say. "It's not my fault you didn't do your work.

Kevin sulks and sighs. I don't care. I'm ignoring him. Why should I work my butt off, and then hand my work to him or anyone else? Kevin's my boy, love him but I don't think being a friend is doing your work for you. Especially when he was out hanging with his friends.

I hand my paper to Mrs. Cutchens. Kristen passes a note to me:

Deanne, can you meet me after school to go
shopping at the Galleria? My mom can give
you a ride home, okay? Let me know.
K.

I write back:

Sure. I gotta call my mom first, but
I'm sure it'll be okay. Oh, I have auditions today for

Absolute Rhythms, so it'll have to be after that. Can you come with me to the audition? Meet at the Annex.

D.

Enough chit chat. I have to focus on what Mrs. Cutchens wants us to do.

"Open your notebooks," she says. "Let's review the outline for creating an essay."

∾

After Advanced English class, I go to the bathroom and call my mom to ask if I can go shopping with Kristen.

"All right Deanne," mom says. "I'll call your uncle and ask him to keep Darlene. Just make sure you are back at the house by 7pm. Okay?"

"You're the best!" I say. "Gotta go to my next class now. I love you," I say.

"Love you too baby. Be safe."

I put my phone in my bag and walk to physical science. I sit down and take out my notebook, ready to take notes on Mr. Diamond's lecture.

I hear a whisper from a few desks over.

"Psssttt. Deanne," Palmer says.

Students are walking in late and Mr. Diamond is taking the attendance so I'm going to see what

Palmer wants.

"What?" I ask.

"Get this," he says.

Palmer motions for me to grab a note he's passing to me, from the student next to me.

"Go ahead and pass it," I say.

I grab the paper and read it:

Deanne, I think you're cool.

I want to know if you'll go out with me? My number is 738-2469. Call me if you want.

Palmer

What! I look over at Palmer to see is he wearing a clown mask or making a funny face. Is this a joke? Palmer winks at me and then turns to open his notebook. Guess he's not joking.

Tall, cute and white Palmer wants to go out with me. I barely pay him any attention in class.

It's cool with me, he seems pretty nice. But I can't date though. Mom said 16 is the age for dating.

Uh oh. What will Kevin, Michelle and Daphne think? What about Kristen? Palmer's her boy? I can't think an answer for everyone else. I'm quite aware that Kev, Michelle and Daphne think Palmer's corny and they don't see why I would talk to him or Kristen anyway. But I can't live for them, even though their my friends.

Honestly, I like Palmer, from what I know about him. He's smart, he's respectful. I don't care about him being white. He's not rowdy and rude like some of the guys at Stonywood. He's a little nerdy, but not totally. He's laid back but confident, without being arrogant. Sounds like I know him pretty well. I would say I'm observant without letting on that I've been watching him.

∾

I catch Palmer after class.

"Hey I read your note," I say. "I'll call you tonight or tomorrow."

"Great, I'll talk to you later," Palmer says.

Some of the girls are staring at me. The ones who are always saying "Hiiiiiiiiii" to Palmer, trying to get his attention. They're not in Kristen's clique, so I don't know them. They act like groupies when it comes to Palmer.

They're staring at me and whispering. I don't have time for it. They're not my friends anyway.

ẽẽẽ

CHAPTER 13
THE AUDITION

Where is Kristen? Waiting for her at the Annex and 10 minutes has already passed. I really need to get to the studio. I don't want to be late.

After changing into my leggings and t-shirt, I figure now is a good time to talk to God. I think I have a few minutes alone in the locker room.

"God, thank you so much for everything. Please bless me to do well in this audition and become a member of Ms. Moshe's dance company. I promise I won't let you down."

God never lets me down. Why should I let myself down?

I walk into the studio and it hits me. It meaning icy stares, icy vibes. Dancers are so competitive. I see some girls and boys sizing me up already. Ignoring their petty stares will keep my focus where it needs to be—on myself. I start to stretch myself at the ballet barre and on the floor. I take a sip of my water bottle. Ms. Moshe and her assistant Deandre should be here any minute. I wonder why Kristen didn't show up? Maybe she forgot. She'll probably call me later.

It's 3pm, now all of the existing members of Absolute Rhythms are sitting in the back of the studio to watch the audition. Talk about the pressure being on. Ms. Moshe just arrived. Deandre starts taking out CD's from his bag. I don't see any drummers so he's probably going to play music from the CD player.

"Hello everybody," Ms. Moshe says. "Glad to see you here for the audition. Absolute Rhythms is a company of students who love dance and want to progress in dance. We are here to entertain and inspire Stonywood's school community. And we want to see which of you will add to the wonderful dance family we already have and carry on the distinguished legacy of Absolute Rhythms. We want to see you perform the routine we taught you yesterday, if you've forgotten any of it, just do the best you can. Now if there are no questions, we'll begin the warm-up."

I take my place on the floor for warm ups and so

does everyone else.

Ms. Moshe puts on Lenny Kravitz's song "American Woman" for warm-ups. Some students scrunch up their noses at Ms. Moshe's choice in music. I like Lenny. A little rock music is what we need to amp up.

"Alright let's go," Ms. Moshe says.

We're led to the barre for exercise and then back to the floor for head, shoulder, and arm rolls. Followed by sit-ups, push-ups and floor stretches.

Ms. Moshe concludes the warm-up with deep breathing.

"Okay shake it off," she says. "I want everyone to line up shoulder to shoulder in the back. Make three or four lines wall to wall if you need to." One by one the students line up. Ms. Moshe calls us to the middle of the floor in groups of four.

"Latrice Evans. Marvin Dullis. Mandy Roland. Casey Frye," she says. "We want you to start the routine I taught you yesterday. Deandre start the music. On count, 5-6-7-8!" Deandre plays Jamiroquai's song "Canned Heat." Ms. Moshe signals the first four students to start the routine while the rest of us watch from the back of the studio.

Ms. Moshe watches the student's every move and facial expressions. I wonder if she expects everyone to be perfect? I see a girl who's a little pigeon toed. She knows the moves but looks like she might almost trip over her feet. Ms. Moshe probably expects to see some excitement and personality though.

High school dance is like one step before professional status for young dancers who may not pursue dance at the college level. Is that something I might want to do? I don't know yet. Ms. Moshe told us yesterday that throughout the years, she found that some kids had what it took, to make it in the big cities as dancers, in companies, film, TV and video, or on Broadway, "The Great White Way."

And if Ms. Moshe could assist the process in creating the next superstar dance sensations, she was glad to do it. She seems like she cares a lot about students. I hope I'll be one of the students she takes under her wing.

"And up, up, kick high girl!" Ms. Moshe yelled to Latrice Evans.

"Good job," Ms. Moshe says. "Clear the floor. Deandre stop the music. Next let's have Eddie Cross, Kaya Forest, Deanne Summers and Tavar Taylor."

I'm on, but I'm not nervous.

"Deandre play the music," she says. "And 5-6-7-8!"

I start dancing and I feel my entire face and head become hot with adrenaline. I'm feeling the music, so I'm just going to let go. And keep a smile on my face. That's something I learned from my teachers at Evening Star Dance Academy. Always smile. Even when you mess up. When you smile the audience enjoys it and they don't even notice if you mess up most of the time.

I'm making sure to stay in the middle of the line facing Ms. Moshe. She's watching us closely. When she turns to nod at Deandre and then both of them look at me, I know I have their approval.

"Good job, " Ms. Moshe says. "Let's clear the floor," Ms. Moshe says. The company members in the back of the studio clap for us. Ms. Moshe then calls the next set of students.

By 4:30 the thirty-five students including me, who came to audition, had danced and are patiently waiting, some sitting and some standing near the barres, to hear what Ms. Moshe has to say next.

"Thank you all for coming out," she says. "Deandre and I watched all of you and we have made our notes.

You were all very good. Just a reminder, we're only looking to fill fifteen slots in the company. If you're not chosen you can always try for next year. We will post a list of the students we selected, on Monday outside of dance studio by 12noon. Also on the list will be the date and time for Absolute Rhythms first rehearsal. Go home, get some rest and have a good weekend!"

All of the students in the studio clap, some patting each other on the backs and hugging.

A short, thick-bodied, brown-skinned girl with highlighted hair pulled into a high ponytail, wearing a white tank top and black dance shorts walks over to me.

"So think you made it?"

"I hope so," I say.

I wipe the sweat from my neck and back with a towel and grab my bag.

"I'm Latrice. I think we eat on the same lunch."

"I think I've seen you around."

"Alright well I gotta run. Maybe we'll both make it. Cross your fingers."

Latrice turns to grab her bag, and walk out.

"I will. Good luck."

I don't feel like staying in the studio to talk to

anyone else. By the time I change in the locker room, Ms. Moshe, Deandre and the dance company members have cleaned up the studio and are preparing to leave.

That was amazing. All I know is I have to make it into the company. I feel my phone vibrating through my bag.

"Hello."

"Deanne, I am so sorry," Kristen says. "I didn't mean to miss your audition. One of my neighbors, Harris, came up to the school to see his old teachers, he's at St. Louis U. now. So anyway he offered to take me to get something to eat. So you still want to meet? I can be back at the school in ten minutes, we're on Forsythe now. How was your audition anyway?"

"It went really well. Are you sure you feel like even coming back to meet me here? I am a little tired, I could just go on home."

"No, no, it's fine. We're on our way okay? So be out front."

"Okay, Kristen. But if you take too long I'm leaving."

"We won't. Bye."

ℰℰℰ

CHAPTER 14
NO SHE DIDN'T

When it comes to Kristen, it's always some sort of adventure I'm on with her. I spot Kristen pulling up with her friend.

"There she is!"

Kristen waves to me, I wave back. She's in a candy apple red Audio driven by her neighbor Harris. Harris pops the car door lock for me and I slide into the back seat.

"What's up. I'm Harris."

"Hi. I'm Deanne. Thanks for the ride."

"No problem," he says.

"So what's up Deanne?" Kristen asks. "How did everything go with the audition?"

Harris turns up the radio, playing Ne-Yo's "Money Can't Buy."

"It was awesome!" I say. "But oh, there were so many

kids trying to get their spot. I'll know whether I'm in on Monday.

"That's great Deanne," Kristen says. "So are you ready to hit the Galleria and shop until you drop?"

"Me? Shopping? Not today. I'll be cool watching you shop until you drop. "

"Okay, well I got you if you see something you like."

Really I can't think about clothes right now. All I have is $7 left over from my allowance. I'm so hungry I think I'm going to use it at the Food Court.

"That's sweet Kristen, thanks."

The ten-minute ride in Harris' Audi is pretty cool. The autumn breeze coming through the window mixed with the sounds of Ne-Yo and Young Jeezy goes with the vibe. Now we're at the best mall in all of St. Louis—the Galleria. Harris drops us off at the Lord & Taylor entrance.

"Thanks Harris," Kristen says. "Can you open the trunk so I can get my bag?"

"Nice meeting you Deanne," Harris says. "Kristen don't stay out too late on a school night." He laughs.

"Whatever," Kristen says.

"Bye, thank you," I say.

We walk into the mall and Kristen spots the pretzel shop. She treats me to a cheese pretzel and a soda.

"Let's go to the Gap," Kristen says.

"I don't really see anything new," I say.

"Me either, let's go," Kristen says.

We see Claire's Boutique.

"Oh Claire's!" We both say at the same time.

You can never have too many earrings, or bracelets or necklaces or headbands. Love Claire's. Kristen gets a pack of stud earrings on sale. Now we're heading to Macy's.

"Let's ask for perfume samples," I say. The make up counters always have extra samples.

"There are so many cute boys walking around," Kristen says. "Oh just remembered I gotta get a new case for my phone. Let's go to Southwestern Bell."

"Cool," I say.

We walk into Southwestern Bell on the second floor of the mall. A boy who must be about seventeen or eighteen greets us.

"Welcome to Southwestern Bell wireless," he says. "My name is Mitchell David and I'd be glad to assist you ladies."

Mitchell is tall, well dressed, with café au lait colored skin, brown curly hair, soft brown eyes, thick eyebrows, a slim athletic build, perfect teeth and a killer smile. Like is this guy a model?

Me and Kristen look at each other and almost can't contain our giggles. Mitchell is fine!

"Uh yeah," Kristen says. "I need a new case for my phone and my friend here…"

"Needs nothing," I say. "I'm fine. Kristen you go ahead and get what you need."

I look at Kristen who's already playing with her hair and batting her eyes at Mitchell.

Kristen and Mitchell are getting along just fine.

"So you go to Stonywood huh?" Mitchell asks. "Yeah my school never plays Stonywood in any sports, but you all always come to our parties at St. Mary's."

"You go to St. Mary's the Catholic school for boys?" Kristen asks. "I've never been to any of the parties."

" I heard the guys there are really stuck-up but you seem really nice," I say.

"Of course I'm nice," he says. "You can't believe everything you hear. "

"So what's your name?" Kristen asks. "Mitchell.

And yours?"

"Kristen."

"Well Kristen maybe I can call you sometime."

"Yeah sure," she says. "I'll give you my number."

Kristen turns and gives me a look like "Score."

She definitely goes after what she wants. I know we have that in common.

"You can put my number in your phone, and I'll add yours."

They put each other's numbers in their phones.

"Hey are you going to buy anything?" I ask.

"Yeah," Kristen says. "Mitchell show me some of the new cases you have."

"Sure, come over here"

Kristen made a purchase and got the digits of a fine guy. That's killing two birds with one stone. I'm not mad at her.

"Oh let's head into Victoria's Secret," Kristen says. "They might have a sale. Then we can grab a bite and I'll call my mom to pick us up."

"Okay" I say.

Victoria's Secret is downstairs on the first floor. As soon as we walk in Kristen starts going coo-coo for cocoa puffs over the sale.

"Deanne look, a sale!" she says. "Girl I'm going to go crazy!"

Kristen starts picking up panties and bras and holding them up to herself while looking in a full-length mirror.

"Can I help you two?" A saleswoman asks.

"No," Kristen says.

"Kristen look at these silky nightgowns over here. Would you ever wear something like this?"

"Heck yeah I would!"

We both laugh.

"So Mitchell is pretty cute huh?" I ask. "Have you ever dated a black guy before?"

"No, not really. I mean I really haven't been dating. I usually go out in groups, but now that I'm in high school my parents are cool with it. And I can't let that hottie go to waste!"

"You are so crazy Kristen!"

They eyed all the pretty, soft, lacy and delicate girl things in Victoria's Secret. They sprayed on the body sprays, rubbed scented lotions on their hands and posed in the mirrors pretending to be "sexy ladies" while holding up silk robes and teddies in front of themselves.

"Deanne you go look around, I'm going to see what I want and maybe I'll try on a few things."

"Sure. I'll be around here."

I find the scented lotions and start rubbing a sample on my hands. I look up a few minutes later and see Kristen from the mirror in back of the store, stuffing sale panties and sports bras, in her Coach bag.

Is she kidding? This has got to be a joke? Why would Kristen need to steal? She said she was going to 'buy' something. Buy not steal. I can't. I will get in so much trouble if my mom finds out about this. If Kristen gets caught, the store might say I'm an accomplice.

I've got to say something.

"Kristen, I saw what you did. Why are you stealing that stuff? You said you have money."

"Shhhh Deanne, seriously. I'm going to buy this stuff okay?"

"I'm not going to jail with you Kristen. Okay!"

I'm about to turn up and it's because my friend is being a total idiot right now. She can have anything she wants courtesy of her parents, and instead she's in a store stuffing cheap underwear in her bag.

96

"I'm ready to check-out. All this shopping is making me tired."

"Oh, yeah? Well I'll wait near the front while you check out." And I mean I'll wait. I'm watching her to see if she's really going to buy.

Kristen pauses and then turns to go to a table in the back of the store. The salespeople have no idea. They're all talking and cleaning fitting rooms. Kristen takes out the panties she stuffed in her bag and leaves them on the table. She looks at me, smiles and then goes to the register.

"I'll take all of these please." Kristen lays out two bras and two panties on the counter.

Thank God! I thought we might end up on the six 'o' clock news tonight. And then I'd get my rights read from my mother, and I don't want that.

"Alright, let's go," Kristen says carrying her Victoria's Secret bag.

"So are we going down to the Food Court now?" I ask.

"Yeah, we can head down there." We take an escalator down to the Food Court.

"I want a soda and a sandwich from Subway. What

are you getting?" I ask.

"Panda Express looks good. Maybe an order of chicken and broccoli with rice."

We order our food and find a table to sit at in the center of the court.

"Mitchell is so hot. He's so much hotter than my last boyfriend. You know Andrew."

"You used to go out with Andrew?"

"We practically grew up together. He lives three houses down from me. But I guess we both wanted to see what high school was going to be all about so we broke up. Oh, I can't wait to talk to Mitchell! Do you think he has a car?"

"Probably. I mean he's older. So you think you might go out with him?"

"Um, yeah! He has to ask me first." There was a long pause while the girls ate and sipped on their sodas.

"Kristen there's something I have to ask you. Why did you put all that Victoria's Secret stuff in your bag?"

"Deanne it's really no big deal. The way they have it laying out on the first table, they're practically tempting you to take the stuff!"

"Kristen, no seriously. You could've gotten caught.

From what I heard juvenile jail isn't a nice place."

"Well I've done it before and I've never been caught. Besides I bought something, it's not as if I didn't contribute to the gazillion dollars Vicky's Secret already has," Kristen says smugly.

"All I'm saying is you could have been caught. I'm here with you and I don't want to be caught up with you like that. Does anyone else know you've done this before?"

"No. And I don't plan on sharing it. I hope you don't either. I just do it for fun. It's kind of exciting."

"There's other ways to have fun."

I stare directly in Kristen's eyes to let her know I'm not playing. I'm not smiling and hanging on her every word. This is not cool.

"Well I don't need that kind of excitement. You're my girl Kristen, but I'm not going down for you on this."

"This is getting boring let's change the subject. So is there anyone you like right now?" Kristen asks.

"Not really. Well, Palmer's nice but you know it's the beginning of school and I guess everyone's nice to everybody."

"What Palmer Pirro! He's my boy. His father owns

car dealerships all over St. Louis and his mother is from a really rich family. He has a younger brother named Bryce and an older sister named Alexandra. The Pirro's are really nice. I'm sure there are so many girls at Stonywood who have a crush on Palm', he's just got that look."

"Wow Kristen, you practically told me Palmer's whole life story. Thanks!"

"No problem."

"I know that Palmer seems like a nice guy and that girls like him, so I'm not really focusing on any of this yet. He's a cool friend to have," I say.

We finish our food. Kristen calls her mom to meet us at the mall exit. I call my mom to let her know we'll be home soon.

Kristen's mother arrives to pick us up fifteen minutes later.

"Hey guys, are you all shopped out?" Mrs. Levski asks.

"Not really mother, just tired," Kristen says.

"Deanne how about you, anything exciting happen at the mall?"

"No, we had a nice time."

What I could have said is, "Mrs. Levski your daughter met a hot guy and she's a kleptomaniac."

But I wouldn't be a friend if I said that and her mom would probably freak out.

"Good. Glad to hear you had fun," Mrs. Levski says.

We pull up in front of my house.

"Here we are Deanne. So nice to see you again."

"Thanks Mrs. Levski. Bye Kristen, see you Monday."

"Bye Deanne. Call me over the weekend."

"I will."

Kristen is a little mixed up, but she's cool. No one would ever know that behind that pretty, innocent face, is a girl who has a problem with stealing though.

I hope it never happens again. I won't bring it up but I wish I hadn't seen it either. I guess it's just a secret I will have to keep. Kristen has been a friend to me so far. What good would it do to tell anyone about her stealing?

℮℮℮

CHAPTER 15
THEY'RE JUST JEALOUS

The smell of baked chicken and string beans is in the air. Darlene is at the kitchen table eating.

"What's up?" I ask.

"Nothing. Eating."

"I'll be back," She walked upstairs to her mother's room and opened her mother's door to let her know she was home.

"Mom I'm here. Are you okay?" I say.

I go in my mom's room and see she's laying down watching TV.

"Yes, I'm fine baby. Did you have a good time with your friend Kristen?"

"Yeah, it was alright."

"As long as you're fine. I left the food downstairs for you. Don't stay up too late, okay?"

"Okay. Good night."

"Good night."

I go back downstairs and sit with Darlene.

"Deanne you want some? Mom left the chicken and string beans on top of the stove for you," Darlene says.

"I'll get it, thanks. So how was school today?"

"Hhmmm, it was okay I guess. Some of the kids at school are really mean, they pick on me. They call me bushy brows and dumbo ears."

"Oh yeah. Is your teacher around when they do this?"

"I don't think she hears. And they threaten me too. They say they're going to kick my butt if I 'snitch'. I hate it!"

Darlene starts to sulk. She's really upset.

"Well tell them to leave you alone, or just ignore it. That's what I'd do."

"But there's this girl named Barbara. She's loud and she thinks she's tough. She throws paper at me sometimes and once I felt her pull my hair. But when I turned around she acted like she didn't do it! But if I hit her then I'm going to get in trouble. And you know mom wouldn't go for that. She'd come up to the school and embarrass me." Darlene stares at her fork full of string beans. Tears start to form in her eyes.

"Darlene you just have to ignore it. They're just jealous. You're smart. You're cute. You dress nice and some kids don't like it. They want you to be cut-ups like them in class. They want you to look bad and feel bad about yourself like they do. Go and be with some of the other kids and just ignore the mean ones."

"Okay. Well I have friends, Tanya and Angie. I usually just stick around them. It's just when we get to the playground some of the other kids come around including those stupid boys. If that girl Barbara touches me again I'm going to smack her! I swear!"

"Look if it happens again, just tell mom and ask her to come up to the school to talk with your teacher. I'm sure that'll help."

"Alright, love you Deanne."

"Love you too Dar'."

Wow. Darlene's having drama at school and so am I. I feel bad for my little sister. I don't agree with violence, but if she really has to defend herself against those stupid kids, maybe just maybe she won't get in trouble. And then they'll leave her alone.

I have to eat before I pass out. I fix a plate of chicken and string beans. Darlene finishes her food and goes in the living room to watch a rerun of "That's So Raven."

As soon as I sit down, the phone rings. "Hello."

"Hi Deanne."

It's Kristen.

"Hi."

"Listen I'm not going to keep you long. I just wanted to make sure you were okay, you know about what happened earlier while we were shopping?"

"Yeah, I'm fine Kristen I just don't want to be around when you're doing stuff like that. And I don't think it's cool. At all."

"Yeah, okay, you're right. So you think I should call Mitchell this weekend?"

"I guess you could call him. Maybe wait a couple of days."

"Yeah, I'll wait a couple of days."

"I know. Well, I gotta go. I'm still eating dinner," I say.

"Okay, then. I'll talk to you later."

"Alright, bye."

"Bye."

Kristen hangs up.

∽

It's Saturday morning and I have 9am jazz dance

class, an 11:00 am ballet class, then a 12:30 hip hop dance class. Darlene takes a jazz class at 10am, so we're both at Evening Star Academy until 1:30. Mom takes us there and picks us up, and then we usually go out to lunch afterwards. The rest of the day is spent shopping if we need anything and doing homework. Mom is pretty cool about getting us a new pair of shoes, belts, hats—whatever we want as long as we keep up with our grades. I think that's fair.

On the ride back home mom wants to know how school is going. We haven't been talking as much as we used to.

"How are you doing in school, Deanne?"

"Pretty good. So far I haven't received anything less than a 95% on any of my quizzes and tests. I'm doing really well in English. And I think I might make the dance company at school. Isn't that cool?"

"Yes, that's wonderful. I just want to make sure you are studying enough. Eating good and getting enough sleep. I know you and Darlene stay up late sometimes doing your homework, but I don't want you to make that a habit. On another note, any cute boys at Stonywood?"

"Mom! I can't talk to you about that!"

"Why not? I'm your mother. Besides you don't think I liked boys when I was your age? Of course I wasn't dating, but your aunt and I had our friends and some of them would come over and talk with us on the porch when mom and dad allowed it."

"Mom, it's just weird talking to you about that. Even though I know you were a hottie back in the day!"

Mom laughs and she blushes a little.

"Yes I was and I still am!"

She pinches me on my arm.

"Darlene what about you. Any boys at Stanford-Regent that you like?" I ask.

"No way. Boys are nasty!"

Me and mom both laugh.

"My girls are so funny. You two just stay nice girls so mama can be proud of you. Don't bring any babies home. I'm too young and pretty to be a grandmother! Got that?"

Mom gives me a stern look and looks in the rearview mirror at Darlene. Oh boy, here we go. I really don't want to hear the lecture again about babies and burdens and being a single mother. Yes I can tell it's hard. I see my mom do it every day.

"There is this one boy that I think is nice. His name is Palmer. He talks to me a lot at school."

"Oh yeah? Well what's he like? Does he get good grades?"

"He's like me, you know he's focused on his work. He's also popular. And he's white mom."

"He's white Deanne?"

"Yes, he's white."

"Well okay. It's okay to have all kinds of friends. You know I never raised you all to be prejudice. Just keep your eyes and ears open and remember, 'Don't bring any babies home!'"

"Yes ma'am!"

I give a military salute to mom.

Thinking about Palmer I realize I'm not quite ready to call him. I'd rather wait until I find out whether I made it into the Absolute Rhythms Dance Company. I want to have something exciting to talk about with Palmer.

ℰℰℰ

CHAPTER 16
RODAN TOURNAMENT

Sitting on my bed listening to my iPod, bobbing my head to Iggy Izalea's "Fancy." I'm just about done with all of my homework.

Darlene comes in my room and taps me on the shoulder.

"Deanne, your phone's ringing," Darlene says.

I get up from my desk and grab my phone from my bag.

"Thanks Dar'...Hello,"

"Hey, Deanne? What are you doing home on a Saturday? Aren't you supposed to be in dance class?" Michelle asks.

"Yeah I am but my teacher is sick so the school called and cancelled. What's up?"

"Me and Daphne are going with my uncle to this basketball tournament at Rodan. My uncle used to coach some of the players. They're supposed to have free food and everything. You wanna go? We'll come by and pick you up."

"Sure, sounds fun. I'll ask my mom. Hold on," I say.

I don't feel like getting up. So I yell.

"Mooooom! Can I go with Michelle and Daphne to the citywide basketball tournament at Rodan?"

"What time does it start? Who's taking you and how long do you plan to be gone?" She asks.

"Did you hear her?" I ask Michelle.

"Tell her it starts at 2, we'll come by to get you around 1:15. Oh tell her my uncle's name is Roy Tibbs. I think it's over at 6, but we might get something to eat afterwards."

I tell my mom the details.

"Okay you can go. Leave Michelle's home number and her uncle's cell phone number on the kitchen table. Make sure you take your phone with it. Charge it up before you leave. Be careful and tell Michelle and Daphne I said 'hello'."

"Thank you!" I yell.

"She said I can go, I need to get dressed so I'll see you all when you get here."

"Bet, come fresh and clean girl. I'm wearing my new purple and white Baby Phat track suit with purple and white Nikes. Looking fresh to def baby! See you in a bit," Michelle says.

"See you."

∾

Rodan High School, located on Union Blvd. is a school that is way larger than Stonywood. A crowd of people are in front of the school trying to get tickets to get into the school's million dollar gymnasium.

"Look at that. I knew we should have left earlier. How are we going to get a seat with all of those people here?" Michelle asks.

"I don't know 'Chelle, let's just get out of the car. Since you have to pay to get in, some of these people might not be staying. I'm paying for all of you girls. At least they should have some free food," Michelle's uncle says.

Everyone gets out of the car and starts walking toward the entrance. To my surprise I see someone I hadn't expected to see. Or maybe I just didn't want to see him.

"What's up Deanne? How y'all doing? Coming to see the tournament?" Jahmir asks.

"Jahmir, hey. What are you doing here?" I ask.

"I'm one of the players in the tournament, this is my third year in it."

"Jahmir, how's it going young man? Last time I saw you was two years ago when I was coaching your brother. Still playing for the Westside huh?" Michelle's uncle asks.

"You know it, I gotta represent for the hood where I grew up? Y'all looking for seats? Cause all of the players get six reserved seats for their friends and family. I can take y'all to the reserve seats if you want," Jahmir says.

"That'd be cool man. We were just wondering how we were going to get in that place and sit down," Michelle's uncle says.

"That's nice of you Jahmir, thanks. Oh this is Michelle and Daphne," I say.

"Yeah I met y'all before around Kev's way this summer."

"Hey what's up. Aren't you playing varsity ball this year at Stonywood?" Michelle asks.

"Yeah I am, can't wait for this season. We gotta good team, scouts will be checking us out too. Especially my man Henry, he swears he's going straight to the NBA,"

Jahmir says.

"What about you, are you trying to go the NBA route?" I ask curiously.

"Naw, not just yet, I'll probably go to St. Louis U. or Mizzou, you know concentrate on getting a degree and then see what happens."

Did he say St. Louis University or Mizzou? I didn't even think Jahmir was college material at all. I thought he was just dumb baller. Guess I was wrong? He could just be talking, trying to impress me. But why would he go through the trouble of talking about college if he wasn't thinking about it?

"That's great Jahmir. So guess we'll see you in action on the court today," I say.

"Yeah man, it's good to see you. We definitely need to get to those seats and get some food. You girls hungry?" Michelle's uncle says.

"I'm starving!" Daphne says.

We all walk in through a side entrance which leads to the gym. Jahmir takes us to the seats. He walks next to me and keeps glancing at me.

"Here are the seats. Ya'll can sit down, I gotta go and get with my team. I'll probably see y'all later."

"Good looking out son, we'll see you later. Good luck," Michelle's uncle says.

Jahmir looks at me like he wants to say something else. He must've changed his mind because he waves and then walks off.

"I smell some hot dogs and burgers, but where are they?" Daphne says.

"The smell is probably coming from the cafeteria. Oh look, they're handing out tickets to everyone. And there's a sign that says we can go to the cafeteria to pick up a plate," I say.

"I'm hungry, let's hurry up and get some food and get back to our seats before the tournament starts," Michelle says.

"Ummm, somebody's sprung...Deanne! I saw the way Jahmir was looking at you girl, what's up with that?" Daphne asks.

"I don't know what you're talking about. You are tripping just like you always do Daph'."

"Keep frontin' girl, ain't no future in it," Daphne says.

I didn't expect to see Jahmir today, but it was alright. Maybe he does like me, but he's Kevin's friend and that's it. Now let me see if I can spot him on the court. There he is number 7.

❧❧❧

CHAPTER 17
EVERYTHING MUST CHANGE

It's a rainy Monday morning. Bus #17 isn't as full this morning, looks like some of the kids are absent. Kevin, Michelle and Daphne are here. "What's up Deanne? I hear you tried out for Absolute Rhythms. I know you got the skills to make it since you've been taking dance for so long. So when do you find out?" Kevin asks.

"Today. I should know by this afternoon. I'm crossing my fingers about it."

"So what are you doing after school today D.?"

"I don't know I need to find out about Absolute Rhythms before I can plan anything this week."

"Oh, we thought maybe you were hanging out with your new boyfriend Palmer," Daphne says sarcastically.

Michelle starts laughing.

"He's not my boyfriend. Why don't you guys cut it out? I don't do that to you," I say. "Whatever D. You're hot and we're not," Michelle says.

"Ladies, ladies chill. D. I got your back. Any of those corny dudes try to step to you, I'll squash 'em," Kevin says.

He playfully pounds his fist on the back of the seat in front of him.

"Thanks Kev'."

∾

Later in Advance English Mrs. Cutchens announces an essay contest for all of the ninth grade English classes. Each English teacher gives the title of their essay contest for their students. Mrs. Cutchens' title is, "A Life Changing Moment."

"Students I want you to really look at your lives and the lives of your loved ones and I want you to write a compelling essay about a life changing moment in your life or someone that you love. If it is about someone you love, write about how their life changing moment has somehow affected you. We're going to start your brainstorm and essay-planning page today. Please consult with me, I'll be coming around to talk to you and help you. The prize is $100 and a lunch with me and the two runners-up. This essay is due one week from today,"

Mrs. Cutchens says.

All of the students look around at each other as Mrs. Cutchens shows the full essay description on the Smart-Board.

I'm thinking about what I want to write. I start to jot down my ideas in my notebook:

My first dance recital as a life changing moment
The death of my hamster
The first time I was paid for babysitting my sister
The day my father left my mother

Which topic should I write about? After a few minutes, I decide I want to write about my parents love story and then how my father's leaving affected us. Wait, this might be too personal. But then again, I want to show Mrs. Cutchens that I'm a good writer. How else will I do this if I don't take a chance?

I start to draft the outline for my essay. I'm going to go beyond the requirement and write ten paragraphs. Most of the students won't write that much, and if they do, it may not be very detailed or compelling anyway. I really want to win this essay contest.

I finish my outline before the end of class, with time to spare to start on my first draft. Mrs. Cutchens stops by my desk to observe what I have started writing. She nods her head, letting me know I'm on the right track.

∾

Later in the day, I put the essay contest in the back of my mind and replace it with the outcome of the Absolute Rhythms dance audition. After lunch with Kevin, I have P.E.

Ms. Schwartz my gym teacher is a short, chunky, squat of a woman, with short salt and pepper hair, pale skin, and icy blue eyes. She wears a bulky sweatshirt and black or dark blue gym shorts everyday. She constantly reminds us that she is "...double certified in P.E. and Health. I've been doing this twenty years and I get paid to make you sweat!"

Ms. Schwartz rolls up her sleeves, revealing fleshy arms and a large sport watch on her left wrist. Ms. Schwartz orders us to organize ourselves in rows to stretch.

"Now stretch, stretch!" Ms. Schwartz commands. A girl with a familiar face who I haven't seen in P.E. before comes over to sit down next to me. Ms. Schwartz watches us stretch and calls out anyone who's not stretching. I keep stretching on the gym floor.

"Deanne, right? You remember me from the dance audition last week?" The girl asks.

"Yeah, I thought you looked familiar. Lynette, right?" I ask.

"No it's Latrice. Latrice Evans."

"Yeah, I remember you. Ready to find out who's in and who's not?" I ask. "Ready as I'll ever be."

We spend the rest of P.E. doing basketball drills and running. Mrs. Schwartz yelling at us the whole time.

When P.E. is over, me and Latrice walk down the hall together, to the bulletin board outside of the dance studio. There is already a flock of students reading the list. Some students are yelling "Yes!" and hugging each other. Others slinking away quietly, crying on some-one's shoulder.

"Looks like the names are in alphabetical order," I say to Latrice.

The list reads:

Stonywood High School 2014—2015

Absolute Rhythms

New Company Members

1. Sirus Bell

2. Deborah Brown

3. Karen Chin

4. Coreen Crawford

5. Eddie Cross

6. Latrice Evans

7. Rebecca Freeman

8. Casey Frye

9. Korie Norman

10. Dorian Reid

11. Renee Silver

12. Laura Simmons

13. Deanne Summers

14. Tavar Taylor

15. Kelsey Trice

First Meeting/Rehearsal for Entire Company:

Wednesday, October 15, 2014 3-5pm

Ms. Moshe, Dance Instructor

"I made it, I made it!" I shout.

Me and Latrice hug.

"Me too, I'm so happy. I can't wait until rehearsal Wednesday," Latrice says.

"I think there's going to be a winter concert, which will be really fun!"

"Well I don't want to be late to my next class, so I'll

see you. Congratulations!"

"Yeah, same to you too. See you in P.E."

∽

On the bus ride home Michelle sits next to me and falls asleep. Kevin and Daphne are sitting in back of us. I'm listening to Kevin's iPod and I close my eyes to think about dancing with Absolute Rhythms.

I hear Daphne start arguing with a girl named Tamala, about a boy who likes Daphne. I turn around because they're so loud. Tamala doesn't like me looking at her.

"What are you looking at you wannabe! Hey y'all this the wannabe white girl y'all. She be frontin' like she's all about Southgate, but 'Chelle and them can't cover her for too long. She be hangin' with those white chicks. She wanna be one like that movie y'all. She ain't gon' say nothin' 'cause she a punk. She ain't 'bout it, 'cause she know I will knock a trick out." Tamala say.

I don't say anything. It's the same stuff everyday on this bus. If it's not me, then someone else is a target. I know if I say something, Tamala will hit me and we'll both get kicked off the bus.

I turn back around, plug my ears and get lost in

Wale's "Love Hate Thing."

Tamala goes back to arguing with Daphne, as if she never said anything to me at all. Before they even ask, I decided I'm not hanging with Kev, Daphne or Michelle after school today. I need a break from the drama. I'd rather finish drafting my essay, work on my dancing and if I have time, call Palmer.

∾

I get home and head to the kitchen. I open the refrigerator to see what's there for a snack. I wash an apple, cut some slices of sharp cheddar cheese and pour a glass of milk. some slices of sharp cheddar cheese and poured a half cup of milk. I sit at the kitchen table and start drafting my essay, in between bites of apple and cheese. I write a detailed account of my parent perspective, of her parent's separation and how it affected me and my sister.

By the time I finish the draft it's 5:00 and my sister is home from my aunt and uncle's. Mom comes in a couple of hours later and makes dinner of corn on the cob, turkey legs, rice and broccoli. I appreciate everything mom does for us, she cooks even when she's really tired. And she doesn't eat sometimes until late so that the kitchen is clean and all of our homework is done.

When dinner is ready me and Darlene take a break from our homework to eat.

"Mom, guess what? No, you'll never guess. I made the dance company!"

I dance around the kitchen and start singing Pharrel's "Happy" song.

"Deanne that's wonderful! I'm so proud of you baby, I knew you could do it. When did you find out?"

"Today mom. Ms. Moshe our dance instructor, who is fabulous by the way, posted the names of all the new company members—and I'm one of them. Deanne T. Summers, dancer!"

"Deanne, that's great. I want to go to one of your shows at school, okay?" Darlene asks.

"Okay, it won't be for a while, but I'll let you know squirt."

I finish my homework and help my mother clean up the kitchen. Darlene heads upstairs to bed. It's a perfect time to call Palmer.

I go to my room and sit on a pillow on my floor. I dial his number, 7-3-8-2-4-6-9.

"Pirro residence," a woman answers.

"Hello. May I please speak with Palmer?"

"Who is calling?" The woman replied.

"Deanne Summers," I say.

"Well just a minute please," she says.

After a few minutes a second phone is picked up.

"I got it, you can hang it up now. Hello this is Palmer."

"Hi Palmer, this is Deanne. How are you?"

"Hey Deanne, I'm good. What's up?"

"Oh nothing. I just thought I'd give you a ring, see how you're doing. Were you busy?"

"No, not really. Just sitting here, watching the Comedy Central with my brother Vincent. I was wondering when you were going to call."

"I've just been really busy you know with school and everything."

"Let me guess. The everything, is Kristen and dance tryouts, right?"

"You got it."

"So, what's the news? I heard you auditioned for Absolute Rhythms. Did you get in?"

"I made it! I'm in!"

"That's great. So when do you start you know, rehearsing?"

"This week actually, on Wednesday."

"So, I guess you're going to be a very busy girl really soon, huh?"

"Probably so. I'm going to be on the Spirit Committee too."

"Oh boy, we gotta go out soon!"

Palmer laughs.

"Okay, what do you have in mind?"

"How about a movie at the Galleria 5 this weekend? We can meet there, or my brother and I could come pick you up and he'll just drop us off." "I have to ask my mother first. Saturday or Sunday afternoon would be good. I have dance class usually until 1pm or 2pm on Saturday, so it'll have to be after that."

"Okay, no problem. It's Monday now, so ask your mom and get back to me in a couple of days."

"Sounds good."

"Well I'm going to get back to watching a little TV before I doze off. So I'll see you tomorrow?"

"I'll see you tomorrow."

"Goodnight."

"Goodnight."

I hang up. I feel my heart literally flutter. He's just

a friend. Nice guy. Slow it down. I don't believe in fairy tales. He's tall and handsome, but he's not my prince. I can't get him out of my mind though. Am I crushing on Palmer?

ẽ ẽ ẽ

CHAPTER 18
NO LOVE

It's Saturday and I didn't have dance class today. The day is kinda dragging. Workout done. Homework finished too. Now I'm bored. I'm going to call and see what Michelle is up to.

"Hi 'Chelle, what's going on?"

"Nothing much, just here babysitting for my mom and watching videos. What are you doing?"

"Just finished my homework and it's only 5:30, I'm bored."

"Oh, that's the only time you call me lately huh, when you're bored? Where have you been anyway, hanging out with Kristen?"

"'Chelle, I've been right here. Yeah, I hang out with Kristen a little and you know I've had school stuff going on. It's not a big deal. I'm still your friend."

"No, I didn't know. Neither Kevin, Daphne or I, have

heard from you in a while. We figured you've gone all Oreoville on us."

"Okay that's not even cool, but whatever," I say.

If you want to come over, I'm not doing much. I'll call Daphne and we can order a pizza or something. Is that cool?"

"Well as long as you're not mad at me, I guess it would be cool to come over and hang out for awhile. What time?"

"I guess in an hour. I'll call Daphne."

"Alright, I'll see you in an hour."

Mom says I can go over to Michelle's so I start getting ready.

"Deanne, please take me, I want to go. I'm bored, take me," Darlene begs.

Darlene sits in the living room couch in her pajamas watching TV.

"Sorry Dar,' no kids allowed today. Maybe another time."

"You're a mean sister!"

"Look I'll bring something back for you from the store, okay?"

"Fine, get me a pack of Skittles," Darlene says pouting.

I shout upstairs to my mom.

"Okay mom, I'm going, I'll be back by 7pm."

"Okay, hon'. Be careful and have fun," mom says.

I get to Michelle's house around 4pm. Michelle's 3-year old sister Deja is asleep on the couch. Michelle's mom Joyce is in the kitchen talking on the phone.

Daphne is here and the three of us go to Michelle's room to hang out. Daphne orders a large half cheese, half pepperoni pizza from Domino's and three bottles of Sprite. We listen to music while we talk and eat. Wiz Khalifah's "Black and Yellow" is playing.

"Deanne we don't see you like we used to. You're still my girl and all, but I know you're friends with Kristen and her little crew. And I hear you got some white boy liking you," Daphne says.

"Yeah so I have other friends. What's the problem?"

"So, is it true? Are you going out with some white boy at Stonywood?"

"I have friends, not a boyfriend. What's the big deal anyway? Who cares?"

"Well we heard that some white boy is all up in your face during class and in the halls," Michelle says.

"Oh, that's Palmer. Yeah he's cool."

I'm trying not to get defensive, but like are Michelle and Daphne dumb and crazy? Stonywood is a multi-racial school in a multi-racial community. It's hard not to make friends with kids of other races, why are they so closed minded?

"Well, I don't know. You used to be so down with us and everything, you know hanging with the Southgate crew, that's who we are. Now, we don't know who you are," Daphne says.

"Why does being down with you mean I can't have other friends? Don't you all have other friends?" I ask.

The fun has officially come to an end this afternoon. It actually never really started. I'm pretty disappointed in Michelle and Daphne and I don't want to argue with them. It's obvious that they think I'm doing something wrong by hanging with Kristen and Palmer. Why it offends them so much, I don't know.

I'm not going to tell them how I really feel about Palmer. I don't even know myself. He's nice I want to get to know him and that's it. Why do Daphne and Michelle have to know all about my other friendships? It's really not their business.

Now we're sitting in silence. Sipping our soda,

eating the last of the pizza, listening to Wiz. They don't approve of my new friends and I'm done with all of their questions.

"Well, it's almost 8pm, I guess I better be heading home," I say somberly.

"Okay then D. Thanks for coming by," Michelle says.

"So we'll see you on the bus D.," Daphne says.

"Yup."

I put on my jacket and walk toward the front door. Michelle and Daphne give me a light hug. Sorry but I don't feel the love.

"Get home safe," Michelle says.

"I will," I say.

I walk out into the cool October breeze. I take my time walking, inhaling the smell of damp leaves on the cement sidewalk. I remember I have to pick up candy for Darlene from the store.

Thinking about Daphne and Michelle, a feeling of deep sadness comes over me about the things they said. They're prejudice. And I'm not. That's a fact.

I like Palmer and Kristen. Why can't Michelle and Daphne understand that? Maybe their lack of under-standing has something to do with the fact that I'm really not trying to help them understand. Honestly, I've grown tired of their gossip, their lack of academic ambition and their constant need to pursue boys.

I knew from the beginning that I wanted to meet new people at Stonywood, I just didn't know who I would meet. I never told Kevin, Daphne and Michelle what I wanted to do, but I think they're starting to get the picture.

ℰ ℰ ℰ

CHAPTER 19
OREO

"Deanne, guess what hot guy I talked to on the phone last night?" Kristen asks.

"Who Kristen? Mitchell?" I ask.

"Yup. And he wants to take me out this weekend," Kristen says bragging.

"Oh, yeah? That's great Kristen," I say.

"So, Deanne. You know Palmer and I ride the same bus together in the morning. And Palmer told me he asked you out. Is that true?" Kristen asks.

"Yeah, it is, but keep it on the hush okay?" I ask.

"Sure. But it's so exciting! Do you know how many girls at Stonywood, even upper class girls, are trying to snag Palmer?" Kristen asks.

"No, I don't. And I don't really care. Palmer's a nice guy, that's all I care about," I say.

"I think we should definitely do like a double date.

You know me and Mitchell. You and Palmer. If you guys are going to the movies, then we can totally do that too. So let me know, okay?" Kristen says.

"Okay, that sounds cool. I think my mother will be more comfortable if I'm with you and it's more of a group date anyway. She always said I couldn't officially date until I was 16," I say.

"Man, you're mom is really strict. Well I hope you can go," Kristen says.

"Oh, Kristen, you know I made the dance company right? I'm so excited!" I say.

"Yeah, I heard. Congratulations! I meant to call you last night but I was on the phone with Mitchell for so long," Kristen says.

"It's okay. So, we have our first meeting and company rehearsal tomorrow after school," I say.

"Hey, I wonder where Mrs. Cutchens is? She's usually never late," Kristen says.

"I don't know. Maybe we should just get started on our essays until she makes it in," I say. Kristen then walked back to her desk.

"Good morning," Mrs. Cutchens says. "Sorry I'm late. I had trouble with my car not too long after leaving my house. It wouldn't start so my husband had to bring me to school."

Mrs. Cutchens starts conferencing with students. Kevin and I are side by side, writing.

"Deanne, when you get a chance I need you to look at this. I'm writing about my little brother having asthma and the first time he had a bad attack that put him in the hospital," Kevin says.

"Kevin that sounds like a real good topic. I'll read it as soon as Mrs. Cutchens finishes with mine," I say.

"Okay," Kevin says. "Deanne let's see what you have here. What is the life changing moment you have chosen to write about?" Mrs. Cutchens says.

"Here's the full draft in my notebook Mrs. Cutchens. I decided to write about the day my father left my mother and how it affected our family," I say.

"Okay, so you chose a very personal matter," Mrs. Cutchens says. Mrs. Cutchens put on her reading glasses to begin reading the first paragraph of Deanne's essay:

Advanced English　　　　　　　*Deanne Summers*

Mrs. Cutchens　　　　　　　　*October 13, 2014*

"A Life Changing Moment: The Day My Father Left"

I have seen a person fight for love, and I have seen

a person push love away. But not in the way you would think. It happened over time. The end of love was coming and we didn't even see it. My parents, Yvonne and Kenneth Summers had a love story that never had the chance of a fairy tale ending, because it died the day my father left. It died and a piece of my mother, my sister Darlene and myself, went with it. And now, although my sister and I have my mother's love and she in turn has ours, there is still and may always be, something missing.

Mrs. Cutchens continued to read my essay.

"Deanne I think you should use a thesaurus to make changes in your word choice. Overall I would say this is a very good essay. Make your revisions as we've talked about and then show it to me again tomorrow. Very good work."

So glad I'm on the right track. I will take all of Mrs. Cutchens suggestions so I can win this essay contest.

Now that Mrs. Cutchens has seen my essay, I can read over Kevin's essay. I write some comments and make proofreader marks on his draft.

"Kevin I didn't know that your brother has been in the hospital so many times for asthma. Is he better now?"

"Yeah his is, mom and pops had to take him to these

specialists who are really expensive. My brother even had to cut out eating certain foods that may be causing it, and they have an air purifier next to his bed at night. He takes medication too. Hopefully he'll grow out of it."

I'm sorry to hear about Kevin's brother. Everyone has problems. Not just me.

∾

Later in social studies, Palmer comes over to me.

"Deanne did you ask your mother about Saturday? The movies?"

"No, not yet. I will, probably tonight."

"Okay, cool. Just let me know as soon as you can."

Mavis Jones turns around in her desk and gives me an evil eyed stare until I notice her.

I look up and meet Mavis' stare eye-to-eye. I'm letting her know that I'm not scared of her.

"What the hell are you looking at?" Mavis asks.

"You're the one turned around looking at me," I say.

"It's because you're talking too loud and I'm trying to study for the test," Mavis says in an irritated tone.

Here we go.

"Are you kidding? I was whispering," I say.

"Well whisper somewhere else."

Mavis is so rude. She turns around in her desk, flinging her curly, burgundy and black, weaved hair.

Crazy. I turn around to see if Palmer noticed the argument between me and Mavis. He didn't. He's busy reading and so is the rest of the class. With the exception of a few students whose heads are either nodding off or face down on their desks, including Daphne. Mrs. Aioli is writing the main points on the blackboard from each chapter for Friday's test.

No one saw Mavis acting up. I can't worry about her. I have to think about my test on Friday, so I can get an A. I'm turning negative emotions into positive motivation.

ᐁ

Thirty minutes later at the end of class, me, Michelle and Daphne walk out of class together. Mavis comes up behind me shouting loud enough for everyone to hear her.

"Oreo!"

All the students coming out of social studies gather at the door.

"You think you're so cute. Well you ain't. And if you stare at me in class again, I'm going to clock you!"

I'm turning around to look at Mavis. She is intent on having a fight.

"Whatever," I say.

I turn to walk out of class.

"What? What? What did you say to me trick?" Mavis asks.

I don't get one foot out of the door. Mavis forcefully grabs the back of my hair trying to pull me down to the floor.

"Break this up right now. I'm calling security. The rest of you go to class. This is just nonsense!" Mrs. Aioli says.

A student mob now forms around me and Mavis. I struggle to grab Mavis' hands so she can let go of my hair.

Students start yelling, "Fight, fight, fight!" Michelle and Daphne are just standing around watching as if they have a front row seat at an action packed movie.

I hear Kristen yell.

"Get off of her!"

I'm pulling Mavis' hands off of me. And we're both on the floor.

"Get off of me!"

Now I'm kicking her to get her off of me. I sink my nails into her hands. Maybe this will get her to let go.

"Trick get your nails off me!"

Mavis takes her hands off my hair but now she's gripping my neck.

Two security officers come in and pull us apart and off of the floor.

"That's enough. Everybody go to class. You two girls are coming with us to Mr. Chamberlain's office right now. Let's go. Thanks for the call Mrs. Aioli," one of the officers said.

"No problem, thank you for coming so quickly," Mrs. Aioli says clutching her pearl necklace and shaking her head.

She just witnessed a very violent scene. And it looks like no one is getting to their next class on time, especially me and Mavis.

℮℮℮

CHAPTER 20
ALL IN A DAY'S HATE

Tears of humiliation and anger are running down my face. The security guards have their arm around me and everyone in the hallway is staring. I see Kristen, Palmer, Michelle, and Daphne watching her.

Why didn't Michelle and Daphne help me when Mavis was pulling on me? They were right there. Hundreds of students and teachers are watching us walk to the Principal's office. I see Mrs. Cutchens with a look of disbelief on her face. I have to hold my head up because I know it wasn't my fault.

We arrive at the office of the Principal, Mr. Chamberlain, a tall black man with a full head of hair, wearing gray slacks, a shirt and tie, and the Assistant Principal, Ms. Owens, a tall woman with a short pixie haircut, wearing a navy pant suit, who looks like a basketball player.

"What are your names?" Ms. Owens asks.

"Deanne T. Summers."

"Mavis Jones."

Taking out a notepad, Ms. Owens began to write.

"So what happened?" Ms. Owens asks. Mavis starts to speak.

"No, I want to hear it from the officers first. And go tell Mrs. Aioli I need a report on what she saw immediately since she's on her prep time," Ms. Owens says.

The two officers give their account, and then one leaves to tell Mrs. Aioli about the report. Just when the officers come back, Mr. Chamberlain opens his door.

"I hear I have two students who were fighting in class?" Mr. Chamberlain says.

"Owens, bring them in. Let's talk."

We walk into the Principal's office.

"Do you know that fighting carries a suspension of three days here?" Ms. Owens asks. "What could you have possibly been fighting about when this is only the second month of school? Well almost the third month? What are your names and tell me what happened, one by one."

I watch Mr. Chamberlain lean back in his dark

brown, custom made leather chair behind a long mahogany desk covered with papers, plaques and photos of his family. Mavis speaks.

"Well she was messing with me and that's how it started."

Mavis rolls her eyes. Mr. Chamberlain looks at me.

"What's your side?" Mr. Chamberlain asks me.

"I was talking to Palmer Pirro and Mavis turned around and told me I was being too loud. She also told me I was staring at her, but I wasn't. She sits in front of me, so it would be impossible for me stare at her, unless she turned around to look at me, which she did. I wasn't bothering her. Then after class she called me an 'Oreo' and then out of the blue, she pulled my hair. And she wouldn't let go of me. I kicked her in the knees to get her off of me. And then Mrs. Aioli called security."

"Mavis, does any of what she said sound right?" Ms. Owens asks.

"Mmm hmm," Mavis says rolling her eyes again.

Maybe if her eyes pop out of her head and roll onto Mr. Chamberlain's floor we can all go home.

"Don't answer me like that. "It's either 'yes' or 'no' young lady," Ms. Owens says sternly.

144

"Okay, yes," Mavis says.

The officer comes with Mrs. Aioli. She tells her thoughts on the incident.

"Here's my report. Girls, I don't allow fighting in my class. You must learn how to solve your problems without hitting each other."

Mr. Chamberlain takes the report, reads it and looks at both of us.

"It looks like from reading this Mavis, that you started a fight, purposely with Deanne," Mr. Chamberlain says.

"Ms. Owens, write both of them up for fighting, give them three days. We can't tolerate this at Stonywood. We're trying to raise fine students and we have a good reputation in this community. If you want to act like a bunch of wildcats, this is not the place for you. We'll send you to an alternative school. You hear me Mavis Jones?"

"Yes."

"Not yes. Yes, sir," Mr. Chamberlain says.

"Yes, sir."

One of the security officers comes back in. "Ms. Owens, Mr. Chamberlain. We have a few students that want to speak with you privately about this. Is that okay?"

"Yeah, it's fine. I'll come out to them. You girls stay here with the officer. Owens let's go out." Mr. Chamberlain and Ms. Owens walk out to the hallway where Palmer and Kristen are standing. I hear them talking.

"Mr. Chamberlain, we want to tell you what we saw. Okay, I don't think Mavis likes Deanne. I don't exactly know what started it, but I know Mavis is always turning around in her seat staring at Deanne and once she tripped Deanne when Deanne got out of her seat. I heard Mavis call Deanne an 'Oreo' when we were all leaving class. All I heard Deanne say is 'Whatever' and then next thing you know Mavis pounced on her," Palmer says.

"Deanne's one of my best friends and she never gets into trouble. She was just chosen to be in Absolute Rhythms, she's a nice girl. I heard the commotion when I was in the hallway walking to my third period class, then I heard someone say, 'This girl is beating up Deanne Summers!' I freaked out and moved in through the crowd to see Mavis just pulling Deanne's hair and dragging Deanne around on the floor by her hair and neck. It was horrible. Mr. Chamberlain, Deanne didn't do anything. I think people are picking on her for the wrong reasons," Kristen says.

"Alright, thanks for your help. If you don't mind I need the two of you to write up the statements you just gave me on paper and give it to me by the end of the day," Mr. Chamberlain says. Palmer and Kristen walk back to class. Wow my friends are standing up for me. Not the friends that I thought would stand up for me either. This day is turning out to be like an old Twilight Zone episode.

Ms. Owens and Mr. Chamberlain walk back into the office.

"I think we should have Mary Jolivette-Price talk with Deanne. Sounds like she's getting picked on quite a bit," Ms. Owens says.

"Get Mary on the phone and have her come and get Deanne to talk with her for a while." Mr. Chamberlain says.

"Mavis you can go back to class. I'll have someone send for you later today. Deanne you wait here for a minute," Mr. Chamberlain says.

Mavis leaves and I wait. A woman I've never seen comes into Mr. Chamberlain's office.

"Deanne, there's someone I'd like you to meet. This is Mrs. Jolivette—Price, your 9th grade counselor. She's here for students to discuss anything related to school or personal issues that you care to talk about. And it would be strictly confidential. Would you like to speak with her now?" Ms. Owens asks.

"Yes, I would."

"Hi Deanne," Mrs. Jolivette-Price says. "We're going to go down the hall to my office. So you can gather your things now."

"Thank you."

"Deanne, after you speak with Mrs. Jolivette-Price we'll talk with you again later about this, okay?" Mr. Chamberlain says.

"Bye Deanne, we'll speak with you later," Ms. Owens says.

"Okay."

I'm so relieved that I don't have to go right back to class. I'm sure the entire student body who saw the fight will be buzzing about it both inside and out of class. I'm just not in the mood to deal with it.

Mrs. Jolivette-Price is a slim, yet curvy figured black woman, with medium length hair. She has a tiny waist, and wears a fitted orange top, knee length skirt and high-heeled boots to match. She smells like lavender oil. She talks with a slight lisp.

Mrs. Jolivette-Price takes me to her office. Her office is not as large as a classroom, but it is carpeted, has a table with a large plant on it and eight chairs around it. Mrs. Jolivette-Price's has a desk, two book shelves with books for teens and the walls are covered with beautiful art posters, posters with inspirational words, African prints and Mrs. Jolivette-Price's degrees, certificates and a picture a man who I think is Mrs. Jolivette-Price's husband, a dark haired white man.

"Deanne please have a seat at my desk or at the table, wherever you like."

She continues.

"So I understand the young lady who was in the office with you, Mavis Jones, has been picking on you. She called you an 'Oreo' and then began to fight you. Is that right?"

"Yes."

"Is this the first time this has happened to you here at Stonywood? Or are there other students who have being picking on you, calling you names like 'Oreo'?"

"Well, Mavis has been like this from the beginning of school. I try to ignore her. There's another girl on my bus, bus #17 who picks on me. Her name is Tamala. She is a bully and a lot of kids try to leave her alone, but she goes after people like me, people who are more quiet. She called me a 'wannabe'."

"A wannabe? What's that?" Mrs. Jolivette-Price asks.

"Well from the way Tamala said it, she thinks I want to be white. She said something about me hanging out with my white friends."

"And what did you say in return to her comment?"

"I didn't say anything. She threatened me and I didn't want to fight. So I just ignored her."

"So, you told me what wannabe means. Now, what does being an 'Oreo' mean to you?"

"I guess it means like 'black on the outside and white on the inside.' Just like the cookie."

"So this is what Mavis is calling you? An Oreo cookie?"

"Yes she was."

"Is there anyone else who has been teasing you, being mean and calling you names?"

Michelle and Daphne come to my mind.

"Well not really teasing, but I feel sometimes like

a few of my friends from my neighborhood are trying to make me feel bad because I have new friends who happen to be white."

"So, you have Tamala on the bus who calls you a 'wannabe' and threatens you. You have Mavis in class who calls you an 'Oreo' and fights you. Then you have your neighborhood friends who are criticizing you for making friends with white students. No one is giving you a break are they?"

"No, they're not."

"And how does this make you feel, all of this, including the fight with Mavis?"

For a moment I'm quiet. I never really allow myself to think about the way all of this feels. If I stopped for more than a few minutes to think about it, I wouldn't get out of bed. I would dance. I wouldn't write. It sucks when your friends turn against you and everything just doesn't feel the same. I didn't plan on not being friends with Kevin, Michelle and Daphne. I guess you can't make everyone happy. After thinking a few minutes, I know what I want to say.

"I hear what they're saying, but I mostly just try to block it out. I don't think I should feel bad for who I choose to be friends with. I don't care about color."

"You may not care about color, but others do Deanne. It is a sad truth. I am African-American and I am married to a Caucasian man who I met in college. Did people try to give us a hard time? Yes they did, and I just chose to ignore it. We have good friends and family who support us and we are both happy. You can't always please everyone else, because there will always be something they will use to not like you and not be happy with about you. I am sorry that these students are treating you like this."

The counselor really understands me because she went through something too. I'm sure that was really heard to hear people talking about who she was going to marry.

"Thanks Mrs. Jolivette-Price."

"Sure. Here's what I think. I talked with Ms. Owens, Mr. Chamberlain, Mrs. Aioli and your two friends Palmer and Kristen before I picked you up from Chamberlain's office. I'm going to recommend that you not be suspended, but that you instead come to see me once a week for a while, just until things settle down for you. Is that okay?"

"Oh wow, thanks. I would like that."

"Also, there's someone I want you to meet. She's a student who went through what you're going through now. I'm going to call her in so that you two can meet briefly."

"Okay," I say.

"Ms. Owens can you find out what class Tiffany Hess is in and ask her to come to my office. Thanks," Mrs. Jolivette-Price says.

"I think I know her."

A few minutes later, Tiffany Hess walked in, wearing a navy blazer, white blouse and matching pleated skirt.

"Hi Mrs. J.P.," Tiffany says. "Hello, I'm Tiffany."

"Hi, I remember you. Aren't you on the Spirit Committee?"

"Yes I am. You came to our table. Deanne right?"

I remember how nice Tiffany was when I first met her. So strange that now Mrs. Jolivette-Price is introducing us.

"Tiffany, thanks for coming. Please sit down. Deanne, had a fight with a girl who called her an 'Oreo' today. Deanne is being picked on by quite a few students because she has white friends. I was hoping you two could exchange numbers and talk sometime. Maybe you can share your experience with her and how you dealt with it."

"Sure, I'd love to do that. Deanne, let me give you my number."

We both exchange numbers and I'm happy that I'll have someone to talk to, a student who might understand me too.

"Alright Tiffany, thanks for coming by," Mrs. Jolivette-Price says.

"You're welcome Mrs. J.P. Bye Deanne, I'll call you and I'll also let you know when the next Spirit meeting is."

"Okay thanks," I say.

"Deanne, I forgot to ask you. How do your parents feel about what you've been going through? And do you have any siblings?" Mrs. Jolivette-Price asks.

"Well I live with my mom, and I haven't mentioned anything to her. I just let her know that I'm doing good in school. I have a younger sister who's in middle school."

"I see. I'll send a letter home to your mom to let her know that I'll be meeting with you once a week. If she has any questions or concerns she can call me. Here's my card for you and one for your mom. So today is Tuesday, how about you come talk to me next Tuesday? I'll schedule you for part of your lunch so you don't have to miss class. So come and see me at 11:05. You can get your lunch and then bring it here." Mrs. Jolivette-Price says.

"That sounds fine. Can I sit here for awhile? My head is hurting."

"Yes, of course. I'll let Ms. Owens know you're going to stay here for a while. I'm going to the office and I'll lock my office door behind me so that no one can come in while you're here. Just make yourself comfortable and I'll be back."

Mrs. Jolivette-Price walks out of her office. I rest my head on the table and doze off.

∽

I wake up and realize I've missed lunch, PE and part of math. My head is still hurting and I feel really tired. I better call my mother. The Principal probably already called her.

"Mama, I'm having a bad day," I say. I tell her everything.

"I hate to hear about this. You know I don't teach

you to fight. It's unfortunate other parents don't do the same. I just want to know you're alright, and not cut, bruised or bleeding," mom says. "No mom. I'm not cut or bruised. Just have a headache and I feel really tired. But I'm glad that I'm not being suspended."

"I'm just glad that you're not getting suspended. When you come home I want you to just rest, maybe write in your journal and just thank God that it is not you who's going to miss school for three days. Maybe that little girl will learn her lesson."

"Thank you mama. Love you."

"Love you too suga. Keep your head up. I will call your Principal just to make sure you are being treated right."

"Okay, see you at home."

"Bye baby."

I need to call my Uncle to ask if he can pick me up after school before he picks up Darlene. I can't ride bus #17. Everyone will be asking me what happened. I can just picture the twins having a laugh at my expense, as well as stupid comments from Daphne and Michelle. I need a break from the drama.

Mrs. Jolivette-Price is back in her office.

"How are you feeling?" She asks.

"Better. I just want to go home though."

"I know. I'm going to write a late pass for you. Feel better Deanne and I'll see you at 11:05 next Tuesday. Let me know if you need anything before then."

Thank you."

Mrs. Jolivette-Price reaches and gives me a big hug, the kind my mama would give me.

"Anytime."

I leave Mrs. Jolivette-Price's office. I have to stop in the bathroom. Check myself. Pull myself together, especially since Mavis pulled my hair and my clothes. I put cold water on my face and dry off with a paper towel. I comb my hair and smooth my clothes down. I take out my Burt's Bees lip balm and tuck my shirt into my jeans.

I lock myself in a stall, I have to talk to God right now. This day has been too crazy not to.

"Lord, please let me make it through this day."

Now I feel ready to go to math class.

∾

As soon as I walk into class I hear the whispering and chatter start.

I hand my teacher Mr. Lane, my late pass.

Whispering keeps going, but I can hear them.

"I heard Deanne kicked Mavis first, then Mavis hit her."

"No Mavis pulled Deanne's hair, then Deanne pulled Mavis to the floor."

"I heard Mavis got suspended a lot at her other school."

"Yeah, she's a thug. I wouldn't mess with her."

"Yeah, what was Deanne thinking."

What was I thinking? No what was Mavis thinking? I gotta ignore these people. I'll never get my math work done. Mr. Lane hands me the assignment everyone is working on and I get started on it right away.

ℰ ℰ ℰ

CHAPTER 21
FRIEND TO ME OR FRENEMY?

I feel like I can face today because I got some good news last night, despite having a no good, terrible day yesterday. Mom said I can go out with Palmer in a group as long as Kristen stays with me. I was like, "Yesssssss." So I do have something to look forward to. Any drama today, I can handle it. I hope.

On the bus, I'm hit with all kinds of questions and stuff. Michelle and the crew never stop. I shouldn't be surprised, right?

"Deanne we didn't think you'd be back at school so soon. How you doing girl?" Michelle asks.

"Why? I'm fine."

"That fight you had with Mavis was off the chain. We thought maybe you were suspended or you just might stay out for a few days to avoid the hype," Daphne says.

"They didn't suspend me. It wasn't my fault anyway,

Mavis started it. Why did you stand there and watch when Mavis jumped on me like a junkyard dog? You all are supposed to be my girls, you just stood there and did nothing. I was walking out with you and you didn't even try to stop her. What's up with that?"

"Well D. it looked like you had it. Mavis is no bigger than you. Besides I wasn't trying to get suspended," Michelle says.

"Yo, I wasn't even there, but I heard Mavis pulled your hair. Did you at least get one lick in?" Kevin asks.

"What Kevin? You want all the fight details? Like this is WWF or something? Mavis fought me over something silly and that's it. All I know is the ones who were supposed to be my friends—the Southgate Avenue crew didn't even have my back yesterday."

"D., don't try to front as if you've really been hanging tight with us since school started. Whatever beef you have with Mavis, you to settle it. Sorry but you've been acting like the lone ranger lately, so what did you expect?" Daphne says.

"What I expected is that my friends would be there for me. But I see that you all have times when you're cool with me and times when you're not. So I guess that makes you 'some timey.' Just forget it. I have more important things to concern myself with," I say.

"Cool then. I'm alright if you're alright," Kevin says.

"I'm cool," Michelle says.

"Yup, me too," Daphne says.

I can feel the tension in the air. You can cut it with a knife. The knife that I feel sticking in my back right now. Now I know I can't depend on these three, dare I call them stooges? Because they're not good for much besides laughs here and there. And I didn't realize that until now. The truth hurts and so do frenemies. If that's how they want, that's how it's going to be.

∞

I get to Advanced English class and I'm ready to put that whole conversation on the bus, out of my mind. Kristen comes over to my desk before class starts.

"Deanne I tried calling you last night to make sure you were alright, but your mom said you were in bed. You okay?"

She puts her hand on my shoulder.

"I'm fine. Mr. Chamberlain decided not to suspend me. But Mavis will be out until Friday I think. I just want to focus on school. Oh and I have rehearsals today for Absolute Rhythms."

"Glad to hear you're okay. So did your mom say it was okay to go out this weekend? Mitchell is cool on double dating, what about Palmer?"

"I haven't talked to him yet; I'll see him later today. My mom said it was fine. She's going to drive me to the Galleria to meet you guys,"

"Sounds good then. Let me go back to my seat since Mrs. C. just walked in," Kristen says.

Kristen goes back to her seat. Kevin comes into class just as Mrs. Cutchens was about to close the door.

"Yo, Deanne, you want to help me with my essay draft?"

"No. I have a lot of my own work to." Kevin sucks his teeth and huffs. I really don't care.

I spend the rest of the class period rewriting my second draft for her essay. I'm going to turn this baby in by Thursday.

Next period in social studies Mrs. Aioli approaches me.

"Deanne are you okay? I was told you aren't going to be suspended for the fight."

"Yes, I'm fine Mrs. Aioli."

Palmer comes in and takes his seat behind me.

"Hi Deanne, what's up?" Palmer asks.

"Oh, hey Palmer. Good how are you?"

"I'm good. Just making sure you're alright since yesterday."

Mrs. Aioli makes an announcement to the class.

"Students in preparation for Friday's test I am passing out the complete study guide for you. The study guide has some of the terms, people, places, dates and documents I want you to be able to analyze and identify on the test. Also, there will be short answer response questions. If you want to work with a partner to complete the study guide over the next two days in class, you may do so."

Palmer taps my shoulder.

"Hey you want to work together?"

"Sure."

We turn our desks to face each other.

"So did you ask you mom?" Palmer asks.

Palmer seems a little anxious.

"Shhh, Palmer I can't talk about that now. Let's talk after we leave here okay?"

"Okay, not a problem," Palmer says.

After class Palmer and I sit on a bench outside the building.

"My mom said it was cool for Saturday. Kristen wants to double date with this guy Mitchell who goes to St. Mary's."

"That works. We should figure out what move we're going to see, and meet at the Galleria around 6pm. We can grab something to eat, go to the movie afterwards and just hang out," Palmer says.

"Okay, I'll talk to Kristen."

"Cool then."

℮ ℮ ℮

CHAPTER 22
SMOOTH TALKER

I can't wait for dance rehearsal. When I get there some of the company members were already there and so was Ms. Moshe with her assistant Deandre. I tie my hair up into a scrunchie. I put on extra deodorant and quickly change in the locker room.

"Hello dear, find a place everyone's just doing their own stretching for now," Ms. Moshe says.

The radio is playing, some dancers are stretching, others are eating chips.

"No food in the studio, only water. You know the rules. We do not want to mess up these beautiful floors that were just redone a year ago for us," Ms. Moshe snaps.

Within fifteen minutes, all of the new company members in my group are here as well as the older ones.

"Deandre close the door and turn on the fans," Ms. Moshe says.

"Hey Deanne. Ready for our first rehearsal as company members?" Latrice Evans asks.

"Oh yes, couldn't be more ready. I've been looking forward to this."

"Me too."

Ms. Moshe interrupts our conversation.

"Alright young ladies, and gentlemen. This is Absolute Rhythms first meeting of the school year and dance rehearsal. Most of you know we have a winter concert coming up. And also a spring concert and I know some of you participate in other talent shows throughout the year, so it's going to be a lot of fun. Today, I welcome all of the new members. I'm Ms. Moshe. I received a BFA, that's a Bachelor of Fine Arts in Dance from the University of Illinois at Urbana-Champaign years ago. I've danced with a few companies and I've had a ball being a teacher here at Stonywood. This is Deandre Strong, he's a senior and has been with us since his freshman year. Say 'Hi' Deandre."

Deandre waves and has a big grin on his face.

"Today, we'll start our rehearsal. I'm only going to teach you one dance today, because we'll have rehearsal again on Tuesday. Rehearsal is every Tuesday and

Thursday at 3pm. We only have it twice a week because I know you kids are very busy and some of you take classes on the weekends. Now I want us to all get in a big, huge friendly circle and stand facing one another and I want all of us to introduce ourselves. But there's a twist, you have to do your favorite dance after you say your name and the person after you has to do your dance and theirs too!" Ms. Moshe says.

A dozen groans and chatter about this name game start. For the next fifteen minutes we all tell our names, do a dance and give nicknames we want to be called by.

After the game puts on a mix of lively music—Janet Jackson's "All For You," Prince's "Raspberry Beret," and Pink's "There You Go."

"Alright, this dance routine is called 'Sass' and I haven't yet decided what song you are going to dance off of for it, but we have this playlist here that I think goes with it pretty well. So let's just have fun with it," Ms. Moshe says.

Ms. Moshe and Deandre split the company in half and they each start teaching us the steps to the routine.

"My god girl, this new routine Ms. Moshe has is grueling. I'm dehydrated already," Latrice says jokingly.

"Yeah, I'm getting a cramp myself. Let's take a little water break, everyone else does it anyway," I say.

I grab my towel to dab my face. We walk out of the studio to the water fountain. Just as Latrice and I get our drinks and turn back toward the studio, I hear a familiar voice come from behind me.

"What's up Deanne?"

I turn around. It's Jahmir.

"Hey," I say.

"Can I call you D. for short? I hear that's what people call you."

"No Deanne's my name. What are you doing over here? School is over."

"Your boy Kev' told me you're here after school, thought I'd come check you out. You're looking real good by the way. I like the way you move."

"Look, I can't really talk. I stepped out to get water that's all. Sorry Latrice, I'll be right there," I say looking behind at her standing near the studio door.

"No problem Deanne. Take your time girl," Latrice says slyly looking at Jahmir from head to toe and then back at me.

"Yeah, take your time Deanne," Jahmir says.

"Jahmir, you can't hang around here. Only the dancers are supposed to be here this late. I'm serious about my rehearsals and I don't need anyone to distract me, okay?" I ask.

He stands there looking at me, not saying anything. Hello anyone home? What is he thinking?

"You kinda fiery, in a proper sorta way. I like that."

"Jahmir, what do you want?"

"You're a challenge but I like you."

"I gotta go Jahmir."

I start to walk back to the dance studio.

"No worries D., I won't hang around here. I'll see you around though," Jahmir says. He turns and walks away.

Flustered. That's the word that comes to mind to describe how I feel right now. Jahmir makes me feel— flustered. He's a smooth talking upperclassman. What does he want with me?

I was already warned by my unofficial big sister Tiffany, about how upperclassman sometimes hedge a bet that they can get a certain freshman girl, mess over her and then turn her loose.

I don't know if Jahmir has a bet on me, but I don't think I want to find out. Jahmir and his thuggish swagger won't leave me alone though. There's something about him, that's kind of mysterious and bad. But I don't know if I can be friends with him. Can I?

"Girl who is that? His body is niiiiiice! And he's tall too—even better! Probably one of them basketball players huh? Girl you better get on that, he seems like he's feeling you," Latrice says.

"Latrice, please. It's not even like that. He's my best friend's friend and he's too flashy," I say opening the studio door.

"Well with all the parties and games coming up, a freshman could get mad respect by dating an upperclassman. You are just corny Deanne, I don't get you."

"Whatever. A freshman can also get played and hated on for dating an upperclassman. I have enough haters right now. Besides he's not even the right kind of upperclassman I'd want to date," I say dryly.

"You're so judgmental and snobby. Don't say I never told you how to improve your popularity around here Deanne. I've seen you hanging around that white posse of yours, that's only going to go but so far, until they get tired of your black behind and kick you to the curb when the next Oreo comes on the scene."

"Wow that's really nice Latrice. Did you come up with that yourself? If you're so sprung on the upperclassmen, why aren't you dating any?"

"Who said I wasn't? I'm already hooked up with Anthony Ritchman, who's on the football team. He's a junior and his parents are paid girl! So pick your face up off of the floor."

"No need," I say. "I'm not impressed. I'll stay out of your business and you should stay out of mine."

"Don't get all mad girl, I'm just trying to help you out."

"You can't help me. And I don't need any help."

"Someone's feeling some type of way. Anyway, we should exchange numbers. I got the scoop on parties going on around town, not just at Stonywood."

"You're too much Latrice."

I'm getting better at my comebacks. I guess I've had so much practice with everyone ganging up on me lately. I don't mind exchanging numbers with Latrice because maybe she does have the scoop on the social scene at Stonywood. I just hope Jahmir doesn't catch me off guard again.

℮℮℮

CHAPTER 23
KEEP YOUR HEAD UP

I walk in the door of the house and crash on the sofa. I turn on the TV to relax before dinner. Mom isn't home from work and Darlene is in her room sleeping.

I think I'll call Kristen.

"Kristen, I talked to Palmer. He said he's fine with double dating on Saturday. So talk to Mitchell. What movie do you want to see?"

"I don't know, there's so much out right now. We could see that new Will Smith movie, or the one with Kevin Hart looks good. We could see it around 7pm."

"Yeah, that sounds good; I'll go with one of those. Palmer says something about meeting around 6pm at The Galleria so we can all grab a bite to eat and then go to Galleria 5."

"Cool. I think Mitchell's going to pick me up, so I'll call you when I'm leaving the house. Let's meet at the

Lord & Taylor entrance okay?"

"I'll let Palmer know. Or you can tell him when you see him on your bus. Either way, everything will be set by Friday."

"Yeah, so you hear anyone saying anything else about the fight the other day?" Kristen asks.

"No, I think people have pretty much moved on to other things. I certainly don't want to talk about it."

"I guess you're right."

"Oh, I met this girl Latrice in dance rehearsal. She's a freshman and she made the company too."

"Well I gotta go and finish my homework. You know the essay contest and all. How are you doing on your essay by the way?" Kristen asks.

"It's going alright, I'm pretty much done with revisions. I just have to type it up. Well I know we both have stuff to do, so I'll see you tomorrow."

"Alright, have a good night. See you," Kristen says.

I'm hungry, but too tired to heat up leftovers. I make a turkey sandwich with lettuce and tomato on wheat bread and pour a glass of orange juice. I sit down at the table to eat. The phone rings. I hear a chipper sounding female voice on the other end.

"Hi, may I speak with Deanne?"

"Yes, this is she. Who is this?" I ask.

"Hi Deanne. This is Tiffany Hess. I talked to you in Mrs. Jolivette-Price's office the other day. How are you?"

"Good, how are you?"

"Great. Just thought I'd give you a call, talk to you for a bit. Are you busy?"

"No, just eating but I can talk."

"Mrs. J.P. told me all about what happened to you the other day. I'm sorry to hear about fight. It totally brought back memories because the same thing happened to me in both my freshman and sophomore years. It was a nightmare."

"What happened?"

"I just moved here from Indiana the summer before. My mom is white and my dad is black. I never thought I was different, but I came to Stonywood and the kids were so harsh, I mean mainly the black kids. I just wanted to be friends with everyone. You know being tall, skinny and everything I haven't always been confident, but I've always been smart. Kids would call me 'white girl', just all kinds of names."

"That's awful," I say.

"There was this girl, Nolita who was always picking on me in the hallway. She had this crew of girls who hung with her and they were so tough looking. They wore these matching T-shirts all of the time with their nicknames spray painted on the back. Well one day, freshman year I was walking down the hallway and Nolita threw pencils at me. I heard her call me a 'white bish.' Well that was it! I threw my backpack at her."

No way! I thought I had it bad. Listening to Tiffany's story gives me flashbacks about Mavis. I can't even picture Tiffany throwing anything at anyone. I want to know how it all ended.

"What did she do?"

"She jumped on me and three of her friends jumped in. I fought, but by the time security broke it up, my nose was bleeding, my shirt was ripped off, one of my earrings came out, my hair was all over my head and I was a sobbing mess. Anyway, the girls were suspended. I was given in-house suspension for one day and a whole lot of counseling with Mrs. J.P. By the end of sophomore year the teasing pretty much stopped. And now, no one can tell me anything because I know I am all that!"

"Wow Tiffany. I can't believe you went through all

that? Kids can be so mean, but you dealt with it."

"The sad part, the girls who teased me so much, they've already dropped out of school and I heard a few of them have been locked up for committing crimes. Sarah, the girl you met the day you signed up for the Freshman Spirit Committee, is my best friend. We've been friends since freshman year. Do you have a best friend?"

"Kevin, Michelle and Daphne have been my best friends from my neighborhood. But Kevin is definitely my best male friend and I think Kristen Levski is my best female friend. Kristen and I just met this year."

"It's good to have friends you can trust. You need support around you at a big school like Stonywood."

"I'm not really talking to Michelle and Daphne much. They watched Mavis jump me and didn't even help me."

"Hmm, sounds like they might not be the best of friends to you. But time will tell, you know?".

"So, do you know when the Spirit Committee is meeting again?"

"Can you meet at 2:45 on Friday in the cafeteria? We're having a brief meeting. Deanne, you have my number you can call me anytime. Don't let the silly kids at Stonywood stress you out. I heard you are very smart, so keep your head up."

"Thanks Tiffany. I'll see you at the meeting on Friday. "

"Great, see you then."

We hang up. I'm still in disbelief about all of the similarities between my and Tiffany's experiences. Why are girls so mean to each other? If someone is so different from you and you don't like them, why not stay away from them? The time and energy it takes to hate on someone and bully them can totally be spent doing other things. I'm glad Tiffany called. It just seems like she's really someone I can talk to when things get bad.

❧❧❧

CHAPTER 24
MAKE A CHOICE

I'm spending most of my day finishing up assignments, reading for Advance English and studying for Friday's social studies test. The whole school is looking forward to the weekend. The weather forecast is somewhere between 75 and 80 degrees, sunny and clear skies for entire weekend, which is really nice for late October. When it's this nice we eat lunch outside on the front and back lawns and benches.

I feel good because I just turned in the final draft of my essay to Mrs. Cutchens on Thursday for the contest. Mrs. Cutchens gave it a once over.

"Good job Deanne. I'll add it to my pile of essays that I have to read over the weekend. The winner of the contest will be announced during first period on the loudspeaker by one of the school secretaries."

"Great thanks Mrs. Cutchens."

Palmer and I study together in science class. He passes me a note:

Deanne,

I'm looking forward to the weekend. Are you?

Palmer

This note is everything! But I can't show my excitement. It just would be too much, even though I can't keep my cheeks from blushing. Palmer smiles. I smile. We're both taking notes on the chapter and finding answers to the study questions but it's obvious we're thinking about the weekend.

I feel daggers in my head. I turn around to see some of the girls from Palmer's giddy fan club giving me evil looks. More haters.

I'm going to be on cloud nine the rest of the day just thinking about going out with Palmer, Kristen and her date on Saturday.

∾

I get a call from Kevin later in the evening. I'm really surprised to hear from him.

"Yo what's up Deanne? We haven't talked in a while. What are you doing on Saturday?"

"Yeah, I know. I've just been busy with school

and stuff."

"We used to talk almost everyday last year. You could at least call to see how my little brother is doing. Anyway, I finally finished that essay. I'm turning it in to Mrs. Cutchens tomorrow. You should be proud of me."

"I am proud of you Kevin. I know you don't always like to write. You're right I could call to see how your brother is doing. Well, speaking of him, how is he doing?"

"He's doing great. He hasn't had an attack in a while. I think this new diet of special, healthy foods mom and the doctor have him on are helping."

"And what about Damon and the boys? Are you still hanging with them?"

"Yeah, from time to time, you know Damon's my boy. Matter of fact, I'll check in with him and see if he wants to go shopping on Saturday. Hey, you didn't say what you're doing on Saturday. What are you doing?"

"I have a date."

"A date? With who?"

"Palmer Pirro."

"Oh, that tall lanky dude huh? Since when are you into dating brothers of another color D.?"

"I'm not into dating boys of any type. Palmer is

in a few of my classes and he asked me out. What's the problem?"

"You're just way out there Deanne. Way out there. Michelle and Daphne are gonna flip!"

"I don't care. Bye."

"Later."

❧

On the bus this morning, I just have a feeling Michelle and Daphne are going to start something with me. And maybe Tamala too. I'm bracing myself for the worst.

"What's white with you Deanne? I mean what's up with you?" Michelle says.

Michelle and Daphne sit in their seats giggling as if it was the funniest thing they had ever heard. I'm closing my eyes, listening to my music. Trying to hopefully zone out.

"Deanne you want to go shopping with us Saturday? Oh no, we forgot. We heard you're already going shopping, white boy shopping!"

They all roar with laughter. I turn around to look at them. For a moment Daphne and Michelle's faces look like hyena dogs.

I can't take it anymore.

"You're not funny. I really don't give two rats butts what you're talking about."

They can take what I have to say and turn it any way they want. Some friends. Maybe they need a taste of their own foolishness.

"You all don't have anything better to do. Michelle don't get me started on you. I heard you've been chasing that loser Donovan, the one who was caught smoking weed I don't know how many times in the bathroom last year!"

"Wait, what! Deanne you're trying to front on me girl, it's on!"

"Deanne, don't kiss that white boy," Daphne says. "You might get disease, the herpes sores around the mouth!"

"If it makes you feel better to keep talking about me and my friends, go right ahead. But don't be surprised if someone hates on you right back."

Michelle and Daphne look at each other and then back at me with the "girl please" look.

"Chile please," Michelle says. "Now we know what's up with you. Don't call us 'til you're back to black."

"Yeah 'cause this new Deanne, is fake."

"For real D.," Kevin says.

"Not sweating you anymore Deanne," Daphne says. "Make a choice. Look at who your real friends are."

I turn back around in my seat. I'm not going back and forth with them. There's nothing else to say. My friends, or who I thought were my friends just became the living dead to me.

I kinda expect it from Daphne and Michelle, but Kevin? Nope. Never in a million years. He's the brother I never had.

Time to take a deep breath. I release the breath I was holding when the drama started. Now I can exhale.

∽

It's so ironic that I'm going to meet the School Spirit Committee after school, when I feel like the spirit in me has just been beat down by Kevin, Michelle and Daphne today. I really hope being with the committee will cheer me up. As soon as I see Tiffany and Sara I start feeling better already.

"Hi everybody. I'm Tiffany Hess and this is my friend Sara. We head the School Spirit Committees. Basically what we do is help to hype up the students at the games. We keep the stands lively. We pass out little school buttons, school flags and we make posters for the games. We also sometimes provide water or sports drinks for the cheerleaders, their coach and some of the players if we have extras. Joining us means you become a part of an exciting group. We will participate in the school parades and we organize Stonywood's Annual Barbecue at Herman Park. We have a home game against Rollins East next Saturday, so we need you guys to help us prepare posters and cheers. Any questions?"

"How often do we meet?" I ask.

"Once a week. This year is a little crazy, since Tiffany and I are both seniors. But one of us will either call you or you'll see signs about a meeting hanging up around school," Sarah says.

"Okay, thanks," I say.

"Now we're going to show you some sample posters we used last year, and some buttons, noisemakers and stuff. You guys can pretty much create your own designs. Try to use words like 'Go', 'Fight', 'Win', 'Bring the Pain'—stuff that supports the team and gets everybody hype. So we set up large poster paper in different colors, with stickers, markers, streamers and balloons and you guys can just go crazy! Oh, remember our mascot is the eagle. We have some eagle stickers, decals and cut outs," Tiffany says.

"There's paint over there. What's that for?" A male student asks.

"You can use it on your posters to make designs. The day of the game we meet down here before hand and you can paint designs on your face too."

"Okay you guys so we'll work for an hour and a half to try to get some of this done. When you're done with a couple of posters you can leave," Tiffany says.

I am geeked! This is going to be a lot of fun. I love being creative. I'm at a table with six other freshman students: Willow Mckay, Torrence Meriwhether, Tamika Strong, Antoine Bell, Macio Lowe, and Dawn Haynes. We're starting to paint, blow up balloons and decorate posters. It's even cooler that we're talking and basically getting to know each other. It's unfortunate that several of us have something in common: we've all been bullied or disrespected by somebody at school.

"I was walking home the first week of school and these three guys, they looked like some of the football players, tackled me, picked me up and threw me in a dumpster!" Macio says.

"I was sitting in a math class one day and some freak in back of me, poked at my behind with his ruler. I turned around and smacked him 'cause I know he did it on purpose," Dawn says.

"I asked my social studies teacher why Thomas Jefferson still had slaves when all the slaves were supposed to be free and my teacher looked at me and said 'don't question history!' I couldn't believe it. I said to myself, 'This teacher is crazy!'" Tamika says.

"My gym teacher is a trip. That lady, Ms. Schwartz, she's like a military man. She really takes P.E. seriously," Willow says.

"Well if I must speak for all the guys, the girls here at Stonywood are fine!" Torrence says. Everyone laughs.

"Well I guess you all heard I had a fight with a girl in my social studies class," I say.

"Yeah I heard about it. What started it?" Antoine asks.

"She called me an 'Oreo'. Then she pulled my hair," I say.

"See, that's when you gotta go psycho on a bish," Tamika says. "Some of these girls at Stonywood are bat-isht crazy!"

Several students nod their heads and laugh.

"How's everybody doing?" Tiffany asks.

"Fine," I say.

"As soon as you get a few more posters done you all can go," Tiffany says.

"Just leave the posters and the rest of the stuff here and Sarah and I will lock everything up over there."

I walk out with everyone and then head to my bus stop. I wonder what Palmer's doing?

℮℮℮

CHAPTER 25
HERE COME THE BUTTERFLIES

I still can't believe my mom is letting me go on a group date. She knows that I can handle myself and I'm with a friend I trust, Kristen. Mom is going to drop me off at the mall so I can meet them.

"So my dear you're meeting Kristen and the guys this evening? What time do you want to leave here?"

"We can leave at 5:30. I think Kristen, Mitchell and Palmer want to get something to eat before the movie."

"I'm going to run over to your grandparents for awhile to drop the sewing machine off."

"Alright mama, see you in a little bit."

"See you pumpkin."

Mom kisses me on my forehead. I'm going to relax for a bit.

Just when lay down on the couch to watch TV, the phone rings. It's Kristen.

"Deanne? Hi, are you ready? I can't wait to see Mitchell. We haven't seen each other since we first met, can you believe it?"

"Yes I'm ready. I need to call Palmer though, just so we're all on the same page about what time we're meeting. So what are you wearing?"

"I figured I'd go ahead and wear this button up denim Gap shirt with my red Guess corduroys and my black leather ankle boots. But the real question is what are you wearing Deanne?"

"A flared denim skirt and a hot pink, ribbed v-neck XOXO sweater, black tights and black boots. I have these hot pink hoop earrings that match the sweater too!"

"Oh Palmer's going to be really checking you out!"

"I hope so."

"So what time is your mom dropping you off at the Galleria?"

"5:30. I should be able to meet you guys at the Lord & Taylor entrance a little before 6pm. So we're going to see that movie with Will Smith in it right?"

"Yeah, Mitchell wants to see it and I think it'll be good."

"Well I'm going to give Palmer a call and I'll see you

guys at 6pm."

"See you...bye-bye."

I'm heading upstairs to my room. I turn on my radio, the sound of Adele's soulful voice comes on. I plop down on my bed and just star at the ceiling and look all around. I cleaned my room and it's finally straight and organized. It's decorated in pale pink and lavender. I love the light that comes into my room from the windows. The sunlight streams in from one window opposite my door, and it hits my aquarium filled with tropical fish.

My aquarium sits on a wide table with an African violet plant and a few blank notebooks that I keep for English. My room is carpeted in soft pale pink. Two dressers filled with my clothes are painted in pale pink. There's an inn table next to my bed with a lamp painted with red and pink hearts on it. On top of my dresser are my lip glosses, deodorant, body sprays, my watch and a basket full with hair ties, scrunchies, barrettes and headbands.

Family photos and posters of actors, singers and dancers like Debbie Allen, Misty Copeland, Kevin Hart, Orlando Bloom, Beyonce and Kelly Clarkson hang on my walls. I also have a Maya Angelou poster with her poem "Phenomenal Woman" hanging above my bed. My white and pink terry-cloth robe with teddy bears hangs from the back of my closet.

The inside of my closet is a different story. It's halfway open, with scarves and belts hanging over the top of the door, shoes, purses and several clothing items spilled out of it.

Now I'm thinking about Palmer. Drifting off to sleep is easy.

∾

It's an hour later and I remember that I need to call Palmer.

"Hello may I speak to Palmer?" I ask.

"Just a minute," a female voice answers.

"This is his mother, who should I say is calling?"

"Oh, hello Mrs. Pirro, this is Deanne Summers."

"Oh, okay dear. Just a moment. Palmer, Palmer, pick up."

"Hello. I got it mom, you can hang up now."

"Hi Palmer."

"Hey Deanne, what's up?"

"Nothing much. Are you ready for this evening?"

Sure. We're meeting at 7pm?"

"No, we're meeting at 6pm. We're going to see the new Will Smith movie which should be good."

"Cool, that means we'll have time to eat. I can be there a little before 6pm."

"Okay, see you there. Anything else?"

"See you then."

"Okay then, bye."

A couple of hours and a nap later, mom wakes me up.

"Deanne, wake-up. Don't you have to shower and get dressed to go out?"

"Yes ma'. I'm getting up."

I lay out my skirt, top and tights on my bed. I put on my robe and shower cap and grab my Healing Gardens lavender body wash. Fifteen minutes later I've showered, brushed my teeth. I moisturize my face, body and hands, put on deodorant and then put my clothes on. Really trying not to wrinkle them. I turn on my curling iron to touch up my hair. I look in the mirror. A little make up? Yeah, why not.

A little blush and some lip gloss.

"It's 5:20pm D., we have to leave soon," mom yells.

"Okay, almost ready."

I quickly curl my her hair, spray a little sheen on it, lightly dust my face with blush, put on my her earrings, bracelet, watch and necklace and now I'm ready. I turn off my curling iron.

I check my purse to make sure my cell phone, mirror, hand sanitizer, and napkins are in it.

"Oooooh Deanne. You think you're cute 'cause you have a date. Oooooh Deanne has a boyfriend!" Darlene teased.

"Come on Darlene, you're coming with us. I'll drop Deanne off. You and I are going to Burger King afterwards."

"Yes! I get Burger King and Deanne doesn't."

"Yeah, yeah, yeah, you know you're gonna miss me," I say.

"No I won't."

"Okay, that's enough you two. Everyone get your jackets, and let's go,"

We walk out to the car. Mom unlocks the doors to her Toyota Camry. She turns on the radio to AM talk radio.

We drive off. Fifteen minutes later, we're at the entrance to the Galleria.

"Okay Deanne, have fun," mom says.

She leans out of the car to hug me when I get out.

"Darlene are you coming up here to the front?"

"No mom. Let's pretend you're my chauffeur."

"Girl, if you don't get up here right now! I'm not your chauffeur Little Miss!"

I get out of the car and Darlene moves to the front passenger seat.

"Thanks mom. I think the movie should be over by 8:30pm. But just in case you can get here like at 8:45pm and I'll meet you right here."

"Okay hon'. Have a good time. Here's $20. Be safe and call me when you're ready."

"Okay mama. Bye Darlene."

I pinch my sister's forehead.

"Bye."

The mall is crowded. I recognize a lot of kids I've seen at Stonywood. I fluff my hair and add a little bit more lip gloss so my lips don't look dry. What am I doing? I don't have to try to impress Palmer. He already likes me. Technically isn't really a date. It's a group date. But I'm a little nervous. Here come the butterflies, having a party and flying around in my stomach.

Is Palmer just a friend? Or could he be a boyfriend? I shouldn't think so much. Only time will tell.

ểểể

Reading and Discussion Questions

Deanne in the Middle is a story about a teen girl who faces bullying and social pressure from her friends during her first year of high school. You can use the following questions to spark a discussion or a debate amongst your reading group. The questions can also be used as prompts for an essay.

1. When you first meet Deanne Summers what were your thoughts about her personality and outlook?

2. Do you think Deanne is judgmental of her friends and peers? If yes, explain why. If no, explain why.

3. What do you think Deanne's father's absence has to do with her outlook and motivation to succeed? Explain.

4. Do you think Deanne's Southgate Avenue friends— Kevin, Michelle and Daphne are true friends? If yes, explain why. If no, explain why.

5. Why do you think Deanne didn't initially seem very excited to befriend Kristen?

6. When Kristen told Deanne that she speaks "very well for a black girl" what did you think about that? Was it an insult or a compliment? Explain.

7. Does Kevin sound like he's going down the wrong path? How about Kristen? If yes, explain why. If no, explain why.

8. How does the theme of bullying run through the entire story? What are the acts of bullying that occur?

9. How do some of the characters reveal ignorance about or intolerance for those who are different from them?

10. What does the term "Oreo" mean? Why would a student call another student that?

11. Who are the characters that have a positive impact on Deanne's life? Name them and explain what they each do for Deanne?

12. How does Deanne respond to the people who disappoint or hurt her?

13. Do you think Deanne makes good choices? If yes, explain. If no, explain.

Have a question or comment for the author? Want DuEwa Frazier to come to your school, conference or library for a program? Email duewa@duewaworld.com for all inquiries.

Thanks for your support!

Photo credit: Tangie Henry

About the Author

DuEwa Frazier is an award nominated poet, author, journalist, speaker and educator. She is the editor of the NAACP Image Award nominated anthology, Check the Rhyme: An Anthology of Female Poets & Emcees and the author of several books of poetry, including Goddess Under the Bridge and Ten Marbles and a Bag to Put Them In: Poems for Children. DuEwa earned the B.A. degree in English at Hampton University and advanced degrees in Education and Creative Writing. She resides in New York. Visit her website at www.duewaworld.com. Follow her on Twitter @DuEwaWorld.

Made in the USA
Charleston, SC
06 July 2014